Murder at Jade Cove

A Cedar Bay Cozy Mystery

BY

DIANNE HARMAN

Published by: Dianne Harman
www.dianneharman.com

Interior, cover design and website by
Vivek Rajan Vivek
www.vivekrajanvivek.com

ISBN: 978-1505333701

CONTENTS

ACKNOWLEDGMENTS

To all of my readers who made this series so popular, I thank you for buying my books, reading my books, and sharing them with others.

To Vivek for his constant support and wise guidance, I thank you.

And to my husband, Tom, for his unwavering support. You've made all of this possible! Plus you've gotten to be a good cook in the process. Thanks!!!

CHAPTER ONE

"Mike, I've got to deliver this cake to Jeff Black," Kelly said, opening the refrigerator and taking out her special chocolate cake.

"Well, I hope you made another one for me. You know it's my favorite and I don't think anyone can resist a cake that rich. I just hope you put a lot of that killer icing on it."

"Sorry, sweetheart, I only had time to make one. Jeff Black is very particular when it comes to food and he told me that's the only chocolate cake he'll eat. Everyone knows he doesn't give out many compliments, since he's not the nicest person in the world to deal with, so it really means something coming from him. You know, tomorrow's the big day for him. Seems hard to believe he's going to have the ranch house demolished and begin building a hotel and spa on his property. He told me Marcy was going to Portland to spend some time with her sister while he stays here to oversee the construction."

"Yeah, I know. That project's really controversial and has nearly torn the town apart," Mike replied. "For the last few months it's almost been armed warfare in our sleepy little town. I didn't know when I took the job of county sheriff I'd be trying to keep peace in a town because some Las Vegas style hotel and spa was going to be built just a few miles outside of town. Some people are really for it and others hate it. Even though I'm not in favor of it, I'm glad a

1

decision was finally made by the County Supervisors, although a lot of people aren't happy with the results. I have to give Jeff credit for sticking with his dream of building a hotel and spa right there on the cliff overlooking Jade Cove and going through all the hoops to get it approved. It's going to really change this area. I sure hope it's for the better, but I still have misgivings."

"Well, I'm as happy as you are it's over. With Amber's murder a few months ago and now this, Cedar Bay has had more than enough to deal with. Anyway, Rebel and I will be back in an hour or so. Jeff asked me to deliver it tonight so he could have it for the construction workers tomorrow. He wants to get off on the right foot with them and figures a piece of chocolate cake will be a good way to start."

"Smart move on his part. I'm glad you're taking Rebel with you and make sure you have your cell phone turned on. Jeff's house is a little remote and I worry about you being alone out there. Kelly, don't raise your eyebrows at me when I'm looking after your safety. Please indulge me. Even though his property is fenced and pretty secure, I'll feel better knowing that dog is with you for protection."

"Mike, you know Rebel doesn't let me go anywhere without him. See, he's already standing by the door." She looked over at the big boxer waiting patiently for her to open the door and take him with her. She'd gotten the beautiful dog several years earlier from the family of a drug agent who was killed while he was on duty. They decided to move and she'd never regretted buying the dog from them. Rebel had been trained to attack and detect drugs. He was a natural born guard dog and from the moment Kelly had taken him home with her, his main goal in life was to make sure Kelly was safe. He always kept her in sight except for the rare occasions when she couldn't take him with her.

Mike was a big man and he filled the doorway while he waved goodbye to them. An easy grin, a receding hairline, and about ten extra pounds made him seem like everybody's friend, however, there was no denying the mantle of power the man easily wore. Everyone agreed he was a man you didn't want to cross, but just the kind of person you wanted as your county sheriff.

She doesn't understand why I worry about her, Mike thought as he walked over to the large chair he loved to sit in and watch the sun begin to set over the bay. *But what man wouldn't? She's beautiful, has an incredibly voluptuous figure, her complexion's like fine porcelain, and that thick, lustrous black hair she always wears in a ponytail or swept up in her signature tortoiseshell clip – yeah, it's nice to be engaged to a woman like her. Every time I see her I feel like I've won the lottery.*

*****

I don't think this location could be any more beautiful, Kelly thought fifteen minutes later, as she drove up the long driveway to Jeff Black's ranch house. *Even though I'm not in favor of the hotel and spa, I can sure see why Jeff and some of the others thought this would be a perfect location.* Towering cedar trees framed the circular driveway that led to the large ranch house perched on the cliff overlooking Jade Cove and the ocean beyond. The cove was horseshoe shaped, about two hundred yards wide and no more than a quarter of a mile in length. Jeff owned the land on the south side of the horseshoe along with the land in the center which was where the ranch house was located. The Bureau of Land Management owned the property on the north side of the horseshoe.

The view from the Black's ranch house was spectacular. Waves crashed against the cliffs and created tide pools that teemed with all kinds of sea life. An occasional ship could be seen in the distance beyond the mouth of the cove, silhouetted against the blue-green ocean. In the winter, seals clung to the rocks while eagles soared above. Mother Nature provided a non-stop show from dawn to dusk at Jade Cove.

Wonder how many people have found a piece of jade on this beach? I used to bring Julia and Cash out here when they were young and they loved it. Not sure there's anything more exciting than finding a piece of jade that's washed up on the shore. The people who come to the spa and hotel will love it.

She heard the roar of the waves and smelled the crisp salt air when she opened the door of her minivan. "Let's go, Rebel," she said as she let him out of the van and walked up to the front door of the ranch house which overlooked the cove. She put the cake down on the porch and rapped the door knocker three times. Lights were on in the house, but no one answered the door.

"Jeff's probably out in the old mining shack he converted into his office. He told me once he spends a lot of time out there. Follow me, boy. It's not far."

Kelly picked up the cake and started walking towards the small ramshackle building located near the edge of the cliff. She could just make out the silhouette of the old building in the deepening twilight. *I was right. Jeff must be there. I can see some light coming from it.* She followed the narrow rocky path that led to the shack and when she got there she put the cake down and knocked on the door of the old weathered shack. She waited and when there was no response, she knocked again. *Jeff's one of those people who concentrates so completely on whatever he's doing sometimes he doesn't notice anything else. He probably doesn't even hear me knocking.* She turned the doorknob, opened the door a few inches, and called out, "Hello, Jeff. Are you here? It's Kelly and I've brought you that special chocolate cake you wanted." There was no response. She walked into the shack and looked around. Papers were scattered all over his desk, but there was no sign of Jeff.

Rebel began growling, moved away from her, and started to walk out the door. She looked down at him. The guard hairs along his spine were raised, creating a wide swath of black. "What's wrong, boy?" she asked, reaching down and patting him. He growled again and pushed against her legs, indicating she should follow him. He went around to the far side of the shack and she walked behind him. He stopped suddenly and backed up against her legs, all the time growling in a deep guttural tone. She looked in the direction he was facing and saw a body lying on the ground. It was Jeff. The dirt around him was covered with a bright red pool of blood. Kelly stared at his body in disbelief. *I can't believe what I'm seeing. He's dead, and it looks like he was murdered. I can see a large bullet hole in his chest that's soaked in blood. I've got to call Mike.* "Rebel, come."

He followed her as she ran back to the minivan. When she got to it, she opened the door, reached into her purse with a shaking hand and pressed Mike's number on her cell phone. A few seconds later, he answered.

"Hey, sweetheart, expected to see you, not hear from you," he said. In a tearful voice, she told him what she'd discovered. "You and Rebel stay in the van. I'll be there in a few minutes. Kelly, do not get out of the van and make sure your doors are locked. The killer could still be in the area." He ended the call.

She pressed the door lock button and put her arm around Rebel. He sensed something was wrong and pushed against her. She wasn't the only one shaking.

CHAPTER TWO

Fifteen minutes later she heard the sound of sirens. Kelly lowered her tense shoulders and let out a deep sigh of relief when she saw the flashing blue and red lights on Mike's car coming up the driveway.

She opened the door of the minivan as soon as Mike pulled up next to her and ran into his arms. Seconds later Mike's deputy sheriff pulled his patrol car up next to Mike's. "Oh Mike, it was awful. Rebel found him. Jeff's dead. He's on the far side of his office, the old shack out by the cliff. You can see the lights coming from it when you walk down the path."

"Kelly, Rebel, you stay here and get back in the van. We still don't know if the killer is around. I've called the county coroner and some other crime scene investigators and they'll be here in a few minutes. Now, do as I say and get back in the van. Turning to his deputy he said, "Rich, let's go." The two of them walked along the path that led to the shack located at the far end of the Jeff's beachfront property, guns drawn.

Kelly remembered Jeff telling her that the old shack had been used by the jade miners who had taken jade out of the side of the cliffs for many years until it no longer became profitable. The shack had been there before Jeff had been born. When he'd inherited the property from his parents, he'd converted it into an office. His wife, Marcy, didn't want to give up one of the rooms in the ranch house in order to provide an office for him.

A few minutes later the county coroner arrived with two of his assistants and they rolled a gurney out of their van. Kelly opened her window and pointed to the shack in the distance. "Jeff's body is next to that building. Mike and Rich are out there now. He told us to stay in my van."

"I think that's good advice. Have you seen anything that makes you think the killer is still around?" the coroner asked, his hangdog jowls wobbling as he spoke. Everyone knew how much he liked to eat and Kelly imagined he was probably enjoying his dinner when he got the call from Mike.

"No. It's been quiet from the moment we got here. Since Rebel isn't growling or barking, I imagine that whoever did it is long gone."

"Probably so, but I agree with Mike. I think you should stay where you are."

Several more sheriff patrol cars arrived. The occupants took cameras and evidence kits out of their cars, preparing to gather DNA evidence, fingerprints, and anything else that might help determine who killed Jeff Black.

Well, it's not as if no one wanted him dead. He had enemies. There were a lot of people who didn't want to see this land turned into a commercial hotel and spa. Finding suspects won't be hard to do, but finding out who killed him will be. No one would ever nominate Jeff for the "Most Popular Citizen Award." This is going to be a nightmare for Mike. I wonder how I can help him. As if he could read her mind, Rebel barked, indicating he wanted to help Mike too.

Just as she was considering what she could do to help Mike, he rapped on her window. "Kelly, you can get out of the van now. I think whoever did it is long gone, plus I need to get a statement from you. Tell me everything you saw and did from the moment you left our house to the moment I got here." He turned to Rich, "Come on over here. I'd like you to hear what Kelly has to say, and then I need to ask her a few more questions."

When Kelly finished, Mike said, "Kelly, did you notice anything about the Black's property, the ranch house, or the shack that seemed unusual to you?"

"No. As I told you, I rapped the knocker on the ranch house door and no one answered. The lights were on, but when no one answered, I assumed Jeff had left them on while he was out at the shack."

"Did you touch anything?"

"I touched the knocker on the ranch house door and the doorknob at the shack. I think those are the only things I touched."

"So your fingerprints would be on both of those. Is there anything else you can think of?"

"No, I went into the shack, but I didn't touch anything. Oh, Mike, I just remembered that I left the cake next to the front door of the shack."

"That's not a problem. Imagine some of these people investigating the crime wouldn't mind having a piece of that cake. I need to fingerprint you so we can eliminate your prints. Once that's done you and Rebel can go home. I don't know when I'll be there so don't wait up for me. Go to bed. You need to get some rest so you'll be fresh in the morning. When people find out what's happened out here at Jade Cove, they'll be going to the coffee shop to gossip and see if anyone knows more than they do. Jeff's wife, Marcy, and his son, Brandon, need to be notified. Do you know where they are?"

"When I talked to him about delivering the cake, Jeff said something about Marcy going to Portland and spending a few days with her sister. I don't know her sister's name, but I would think it would be on the contact list on Jeff's computer or his cell phone. There might even be an address book in the ranch house. As for Brandon, I haven't seen him since he started classes at Oregon State."

"All right. I'll make some calls and see if I can find out where both of them are. You know as well as I do that word of Jeff's death will be all over the county in a matter of hours. The rumor mill in these parts is about as fast as the Internet."

"Are you going to have someone here in the morning?" Kelly asked. "I'm thinking all of those construction people are going to show up to start bulldozing the house and getting ready to build the hotel and spa project. With Jeff's death, I wouldn't think it could be started."

"I'll go through the files I saw on his desk in the shack. From a quick glance at the papers, it looked like they dealt with the project. I'm sure the name of the general contractor will be in the files. I'll call him and you're right, the project can't be started since the house and all the surrounding area is now involved in an active crime scene investigation and off limits to everyone, including the contractors. I don't know what's going to happen. This is a real mess."

"I was thinking the same thing, Mike. I wonder if Marcy will continue with the hotel and spa project. I remember you found out that Jeff was the sole owner of the property when you were doing research about the property before you arrested him for growing marijuana. You and I were both sort of surprised that Marcy's name wasn't on the title to the property. I wonder what's in his will. She may not even be the new owner of the property. This is going to be very interesting."

"I have no idea. If everything hadn't burned down in the fire at the back of the property, he'd probably still be alive, but of course he'd be in prison."

Kelly looked up at him. "You know, it's kind of ironic that after the fire, the District Attorney wouldn't prosecute him. He said he couldn't prove that Jeff was growing marijuana because it all burned up. Instead, several months later, Jeff's murdered on the property where he was going to build a hotel and spa that was opposed by many people in the community. In prison or dead? I'm not sure that's much of a choice, but it looks like it wasn't his choice to make."

Mike kissed Kelly on the cheek and opened the door of her van for her. As she and Rebel drove back to town one question after another came to her mind. *Who did it? Why did they do it? Why now? Wonder if Marcy will get the property? What about Brandon? Wonder if the hotel and spa will ever be built?* Her mind felt like it was permanently on fast forward and wouldn't stop.

Kelly had a hard time going to sleep that night and when she finally did, it was a fitful and restless sleep. When her alarm buzzed the next morning, she reached her hand out for Mike. His side of the bed was empty. Her night had been long, but his must have been much longer.

CHAPTER THREE

Roxie, the long-time waitress at Kelly's Koffee Shop, and Madison, who worked there when she wasn't attending classes at the cosmetology school in Sunset Bay, were waiting by the front door of Kelly's Koffee Shop when Kelly parked her minivan in her usual spot.

The coffee shop was located on the pier that jutted out into Cedar Bay. Kelly's grandparents had originally built it and Kelly and her husband took over when her parents retired. After her husband, Mark, had died at an early age of cancer, Kelly had run it by herself. It had supported Kelly and her children through the years and she still felt as attached to it as she had when her grandmother had lovingly and with a great deal of patience, taught her how to cook at the coffee shop. She let Rebel out and he bounded along the pier to where the two employees were standing, hoping for an ear scratch. They both bent down and obliged.

"So, is it true Jeff Black was murdered last night?" Roxie asked as Kelly opened the door of the coffee shop.

"Good grief! How did you find out? It hasn't even been twelve hours," Kelly said.

"Kelly, you know the drums start beating in this town the minute something really good or really bad happens. Someone told someone and it went from there. Do you know what happened? Any truth to the rumor that you were the one who found him?"

"I don't know anything other than yes, I found him when I went out there to deliver a chocolate cake he'd ordered. Beyond that, you'll have to ask Mike. He never came home last night, so I'm hoping he found out something. Come on, this will probably be a busy morning. I'll bet half the town will stop by to gossip about what happened to Jeff."

A few minutes later, Charlie, the fry cook and son of Chief Many Trees, opened the coffee shop door and hurried over to her. Charlie still resented the United States government for taking away his tribe's ancient land. Sullen and angry as always, he was dressed in jeans and a blue denim shirt and wore a large green turquoise cluster bracelet with a matching pendant. The lines around his mouth were deeply etched from constantly scowling. "Kelly, we heard that Jeff Black was murdered last night and that you were the one who found him. Everyone on the reservation hopes it's true. Now maybe that land our tribe fought so hard to keep from being developed will stay as it is. You know we consider that land to be sacred because our ancient burial grounds are on it. Is it true? Is Jeff Black really dead?"

"Yes, Charlie, it's true and I don't know what's going to happen to that land. We can talk later, but right now I expect we'll have a big crowd this morning, so I need you to get in the kitchen and set up for the onslaught. We open in thirty minutes and I want everyone to be ready."

Several hours later she was filling up a small coffee pot from the large commercial coffee urn in the kitchen when Roxie stuck her head in the kitchen. "Kelly, Mike's here. He asked if you could come out and talk to him for a minute and you better take a cup of coffee with you. From the looks of him, he could use a lot of coffee and some food as well."

Kelly walked over to the booth where Mike was sitting and put a cup of steaming hot coffee in front of him with two cubes of sugar and a little cream, just the way he liked it. "Mike, I was worried when

I woke up this morning and you weren't there. What have you found out?"

"It was a long night, Kelly. Marcy's sister's telephone number was in Jeff's contacts list on his computer. I called her and she told me she had the number of the hotel where Marcy was staying in Portland and would call her. That surprised me because I thought Jeff had told you she was going to stay with her sister. Anyway, I would have preferred to tell Marcy in person, but I was afraid she'd hear it on the news before I could get there. Her sister called me back a little later and told me Marcy had taken it well and would be coming back today to Cedar Bay to make the necessary funeral arrangements.

"I also found Brandon's contact information. He's living in a dormitory at Oregon State. I called the resident adviser at the dormitory and told him I was on my way to Corvallis to tell Brandon about his father. Fortunately traffic was light and I was able to get there in an hour and a half. Telling a young man his father has been murdered when only a few months ago the woman he loved was also murdered is pretty high on my list of things I never want to do again."

"Oh Mike, that must have been horrible for you, but there's no question you did the right thing," she said, putting her hand on his arm and patting it.

"May have been, but it sure didn't make it any easier. I called Marcy's sister back this morning and she told me Brandon was going to drive home to help Marcy make the funeral arrangements. Her sister is also going to drive here and stay with Marcy for a couple of days."

The swinging doors of the kitchen opened and Charlie came through them and walked over to where Mike was sitting. "So, is it true that the man who tried to defile our sacred tribal land is dead? Sure hope so. He was an evil man. Serves him right. The tribe's thinking about having a smoke dance ceremony out at the reservation to celebrate his death."

Roxie walked out from the kitchen and put a plate in front of Mike with a big slice of the daily special, the breakfast tart, and the coffee shop's famous caramel coffee rolls.

"Thanks, Roxie. I was thinking about that tart on the way over here. It's one of my favorites. I mean, who can resist a tart with cheese, eggs, and bacon in it? And caramel rolls. This man is going to leave here a lot happier than when he came in, believe me."

He turned back to Charlie. "Charlie, the decision to allow the hotel and spa to be built was made by the County Supervisors. Jeff had the right to build it on his land, even if it had been the tribe's a long time ago."

"Just because some politicians say it's okay, doesn't make it right. In fact, the Great Spirit knows it's wrong. That's probably why Jeff Black is dead. The Great Spirit took care of something the politicians screwed up."

"Do you know anything about who might have killed him?" Mike asked.

A snide smile replaced his customary scowl and he said, "Nope, but I'd like to shake the hand of the man or woman who did it."

"Charlie, think I better come out to the reservation and talk to you and your dad. The two of you might know something that could help me in the investigation."

"Sure. I'll tell Dad. Look forward to it. Might even get Lisa Many Horses to make you some of her famous fry bread. People drive for miles to get it. Kelly won't let me make it here." He turned and walked back into the kitchen. Kelly and Mike exchanged knowing looks and Mike shook his head.

"Kelly, I don't know where to begin. There are probably more people who wanted to see Jeff dead than people who wanted to see him alive. I have an appointment with Lem Bates at 1:00 this afternoon. He was Jeff's attorney and maybe Jeff told him something that might help me with the investigation. Anyway, it's a place to start. Right now I'm going home and try to get a little sleep. See you tonight." He walked over to the door and retrieved his signature white Stetson hat from the coat rack. He bent down for a moment to scratch Rebel's ears, and then he stood up, opened the door, and walked down the pier to his sheriff's car.

"Kelly, you don't think the tribe had anything to do with the murder do you?" Roxie asked.

"I have no idea. Oh swell, here comes Chief Many Trees right now, your favorite customer."

"You saw him first. You get him," Roxie said. "Some days I just can't deal with him and today's one of those days.

The chief stood just inside the door and motioned to Kelly. She walked over to him. He was wearing a silver wrist cuff with a large piece of jade inlaid in it, a jade and silver ring, as well as jade points on his bolo tie. "Chief, you can take any of the empty tables. I'll be with you in a minute to get your order."

"Not here to eat," the chief said in a gruff angry voice. "We're having a special tribal council meeting tonight. Tribe's pretty nervous about what's going to happen to the Black property now that Jeff Black is dead. Some people want to have a celebration, but I thought I better call a meeting before somebody goes and does something stupid. Was wondering if you could bring us some of those special bacon chocolate chip cookies you make."

"Sure. I have some in the freezer. How many do you want?"

"Well, we've got nine members on the tribal council, so a couple of dozen should do it." He looked at the sweet roll dripping with caramel sauce that Roxie was serving to a customer. "If you've got any of those sweet rolls left over, bring those too."

"Okay. I'll probably be there about three this afternoon. I've never been on the reservation. Where should I go when I get there?"

"You'll see some buildings at the end of the road. I'll be watching for you. See you then."

CHAPTER FOUR

About fifteen miles north of Cedar Bay, Kelly turned onto the dirt road leading to the reservation. In the distance she saw a ramshackle cluster of mobile homes, old cars, and a couple of dilapidated buildings. Chief Many Trees had told her that once there were nearly four hundred members of the tribe living in the surrounding area, but now there were less than sixty. He'd explained to her that the tribe was losing most of the younger members to jobs in the cities. Several of them had received scholarships to universities and once they had their degree, they had no desire to return to the reservation with its very limited opportunities.

Chief Many Trees heard her car as she approached and walked out of one of the buildings, motioning for her to park in front of it. He walked over to her car and said, "Can I help you bring in the stuff?"

"Absolutely, just let me pop the trunk so you can get the cookies and caramel rolls out. Do you have any objection to Rebel coming in with me?"

"No. We've got a lot of dogs here on the reservation, although I think they're all pretty much mutts, but doesn't matter, they're still good dogs."

She followed him into the nondescript forlorn looking building. The chief noticed Kelly looking around and said, "We don't have much money and as I told you, the tribe is getting smaller every year." The room had minimal furniture and was cold and uninviting. Nine fold up chairs had been placed in a circle near the center of the room. He looked around, put up his hands as if he was surrendering, and said, "Sometimes I think maybe we should accept the deal offered to us by those people who keep coming here from Las Vegas. They want to build a casino on the reservation. They tell us it would be very popular because it's close to the ocean and it's in a tourist area. If we accepted their offer they said all the tribal members would probably become millionaires."

"Why hasn't the tribe agreed to it?" Kelly asked, her eyes sweeping the bare room.

"Probably because I'm the chief and I'm against it. We have enough trouble with alcohol and domestic abuse on the reservation. I'm not sure it would do our tribe any good if we got rich and then added another thing that could cause problems for our members – gambling, plus it would just provide more money for the members to buy alcohol. I think the tribe should stick to our traditional old ways and not get involved in gambling. When I'm gone it will probably happen. A lot of the members of the tribe are for it."

"If they're in favor of building a casino here on the reservation, why were they so opposed to Jeff building a hotel and spa on his property at Jade Cove? It seems to me they're kind of like the same thing. Both would attract a lot of tourists and I thought that was one of the reasons your tribe was against it."

"Yes and no. You see, Jeff's land is located on our ancient tribal burial grounds. Many years ago, the Bureau of Land Management took that land away from us and gave us this land in return for it. A few years ago the BLM decided to sell some of the land they had previously taken from us. My son, Charlie, and some of the other members of the tribe still resent it. Anyway, the tribe had some money from reparations the government gave us years ago as well as money some of the members had earned when they worked with the miners at Jade Cove. By the way, a lot of our members continued to find jade there after the big mining company no longer found it profitable to maintain their mining operation at Jade Cove.

"When the BLM decided to sell the land, they held an open Internet auction for the property. The bidding was to close at 5:00 p.m. on a Friday. Naturally we bid on the land and were practically guaranteed that we could get our ancient burial grounds back. At two minutes before 5:00 p.m. on the last day of the auction, Jeff Black bid one hundred dollars more than we had bid. We had two minutes to submit a larger bid, but it required the approval of the tribal council and being Friday, many of them had gone off the reservation to Cedar Bay and Sunset Bay. We don't sell alcohol on the reservation, but on the weekends a lot of our members go to those two towns to get it. Anyway, I couldn't get a majority of our tribal council together to authorize a higher bid and I couldn't do it without their approval, so we lost the land to Jeff Black. To say that members of the tribe have hated him ever since that day would be an understatement. Before he bought the land, we used to have access to Jade Cove, but when it became his, we couldn't even get to the beach to mine the jade."

"Well, I can understand your dislike for Jeff Black. It seems like kind of a dirty trick and an underhanded thing for Jeff to have done."

"Yeah, that was just one of the sneaky tricks he pulled on us. He accused us of rustling his cattle, then we found out he was growing marijuana on his land. A few of our young people were buying it from one of his guards on the property. We're pretty sure Jeff knew and allowed it."

"Well, maybe that fire on his property awhile back was a good thing if it destroyed the supply, although he claimed he was growing it for medicinal purposes."

The chief laughed bitterly. "He may have said that, but our reservation butts up to the back of his property on this side of the highway. Some of the members told me they saw trucks going in and out of that property all day and night and they sure didn't look like they were any kind of medical trucks. Heard that the people who drove the trucks were all Mexicans, probably members of some drug cartel. I think it's a good thing he's dead. He was an evil man."

"Well, that may be so, but nobody deserves to be murdered."

"Kelly, that's a matter of opinion. And trust me, your opinion would definitely be in the minority around here. Now what do I owe you?"

He paid her and they walked out to her van. She stopped for a moment, looking at some of the mobile homes which were badly in need of repair and practically falling apart. Those, along with the unpaved parking area and the abandoned cars, meant just one thing to Kelly, poverty.

"Chief, it's none of my business, but are you sure you're doing the right thing by not building the casino on the reservation? It seems to me that the tribal members sure could use the extra money. I've heard that some tribes that have built casinos on their reservations have been able to build schools and medical facilities as well as bring in psychologists to help the members deal with issues involving alcohol and spousal abuse. All of those benefits were paid for with the profits from the casino."

"Kelly, there are nights I don't sleep because I'm thinking the same thing. My time is coming to an end here on Mother Earth and I'll soon be with the Great Spirit. When I'm gone, I'm sure that will happen and you can judge if it was the right decision. Thanks for bringing me the cookies and caramel rolls."

"Chief, seems to me I remember some Native American saying about not knowing what another man is going through until you walk in his moccasins. Don't think I'd want to be walking in yours right now. You're bearing a heavy burden. See you at the coffee shop and tell Charlie hello for me. Come on, Rebel," she said. Rebel was busy playing tag with some newfound four-legged friends, but he came immediately when she called.

As she was opening the door of her minivan for Rebel, a thought occurred to her. She turned around and said, "Chief, you mentioned that alcohol isn't sold on the reservation. Are guns allowed?"

"No. Many years ago the Tribal Council decided that nothing good would come from having guns on the reservation, particularly when we have such a problem with alcohol abuse. We have a strict policy that no firearms are allowed on the reservation. If one is found in the possession of a tribal member, that person is banished from the tribe and not allowed to live on the reservation. Why do you ask?"

"Jeff Black was killed by a gun."

"Well, I guess that puts the members of our tribe in the clear."

She waved goodbye and headed down the dirt road to the highway. *Maybe yes, maybe no. I'm sure if a member of the tribe wanted to get a gun, he could, but it probably does eliminate a lot of the tribal members.*

CHAPTER FIVE

"Rebel, we're going to pass right by the lane where Doc lives. Think we'll pay him a visit. I haven't really had a chance to talk to him about his volunteer work at the clinic and I'm curious how it's going. Anyway, he usually has a little filet mignon treat for you. What do you think?"

Kelly could swear Rebel understood everything she said to him, which was one reason why she talked to him a lot. When he heard the words "Doc" and "filet mignon," his short little tail wagged in anticipation and he pawed at the seat upholstery, indicating he would be thrilled to go see Doc and hopefully get a few pieces of filet mignon.

Doc had moved to Cedar Bay three years earlier and purchased a small ranchette a few miles out of town. He kept to himself and no one knew much about him other than he ate lunch, Monday through Friday, at Kelly's Koffee Shop. Kelly was one of the few people Doc was friendly with and he had a reputation among the townspeople of being a loner, a man who wanted to isolate himself from people and more or less live off the grid.

When she pulled into Doc's driveway she saw the grizzled older man in a flannel shirt and jeans standing near the side of his house, watering his fruit trees. "Doc, I need you to come to my house and take care of my fruit trees. Those are some of the healthiest trees I've ever seen. What's your secret?"

"Afternoon, Kelly, Rebel. If I had a secret it would be loving neglect. I think too many people overwater and fuss over them too much. These trees just like some sun, a little water, and maybe they know how much I like to eat their fruit. I was just finishing up. Come on in." He held the door open for them. "So, what brings you out this way? And I don't see any coffee shop treats for me, so I guess there's no ulterior motive in your visit this time."

They both were quiet for a moment, thinking back to the last time she'd paid Doc a visit. Kelly had gone to his home under the pretext of wanting to give him some food from the coffee shop, but the real reason had been to find out more about the relationship between Doc and Amber, the young woman who had been murdered and whose body had been dumped in the ocean. Madison's father thought he had a large fish on his line when he was shore fishing, but it turned out to be Amber. When Kelly went to the marina to confront the suspected killer, she and Rebel had almost gotten killed after she'd promised Doc she wouldn't go there without Mike. She well remembered internally crossing her fingers when she told Doc she wouldn't go alone, even though she knew she was telling him a lie. She and Rebel probably owed Doc their lives. If Doc hadn't called Mike and the two of them hadn't gone immediately to the marina, who knows how it might have ended, but probably not well for Kelly and Rebel.

"No ulterior motive, Doc. I just wanted to see how you were getting along at the clinic. Are you enjoying counseling people? I talked to Liz the other day and she's thrilled you're working there. Says it makes her job as the town shrink a lot easier."

"She's really easy to be around. Since I'm volunteering my time and not giving medical advice, per se, I don't need to have a medical license. I tell people I'm just a retired doctor who wants to give something back to the community and that seems to be good enough for them. No need for them to know the California State Medical Board pulled my license. Seems that no matter where you go, people have problems, so I'm glad I'm able to help in some small way."

"I'm sure you do, Doc."

"The patients Liz refers to me generally have a problem with some type of substance abuse, like alcohol or drugs. I've even counseled people on the best ways to stop smoking. Next week we're starting a group therapy class for people who are interested in talking about their problems with other people. Been my experience that being accountable and having people care about whether or not you're able to quit something that's not good for you can make the difference between being a success or a failure."

"I'm so glad you're doing this. I thought you'd be perfect for it. Liz also told me she's really become dependent on your advice."

"Glad to hear that. I'm there just a couple of days a week and then only for a few hours. Oh, by the way, I don't know if Madison told you, but her father has quit drinking. He came to the clinic one day and asked for me. I was surprised because I'd never met him. Evidently Madison asked him to go see me because she was afraid of him when he drank too much. I guess he'd hit her a couple of times. I assumed you and she had talked and that's where he'd gotten my name. Anyway, he came to my office at the clinic and we had a long talk. He told me he wanted to stop drinking, that it was hurting his relationship with his daughter, Madison, and she was all he had. He said he didn't know how to stop. I gave him a lot of information about it and told him I'd like to see him once a week. From what he's told me, he stopped drinking that day and hasn't had one drop of alcohol since then. It's been several weeks now and according to him, his relationship with Madison has really improved. I'm glad. They're both good people."

"Thanks, Doc. I know one of the reasons you agreed to donate your time was because I asked you to do it. I'm so glad you're getting some benefit from it, and I'm sure you're really helping people."

"Yeah, well not always. Since Jeff Black is dead, I believe I can talk to you about him. I think the old saying of lawyers, 'that the attorney-client privilege dies with the death of the deceased client,' works here as well."

"I don't understand. What do you mean? Do you know something about Jeff Black? Why would he go to see you?"

"The answer to your first question is yes, I do know a little about Jeff. I don't think it's common knowledge in town, at least I never heard anyone talk about it, but Jeff was pretty sure his wife was having an affair with some guy named Gabe Lewis. Guess he's a big lumber honcho up in Sunset Bay."

"You're kidding! Marcy and Gabe? Wow! I've never met him, but I hear he's probably the richest guy around in these parts. He owns thousands of acres of cedar trees and also the big lumber mill where every cedar tree you see on a logging truck around here goes to be processed. His family started in the lumber business well over a hundred years ago and he runs it now. Marcy likes the good life and has expensive tastes, but I can't figure out why she'd risk Jeff finding out about it. He gave her whatever she wanted and next to Gabe, he's probably, or was, the second richest man in the county."

"Well, Jeff was thinking about divorcing her. When I saw him, a couple of days before he was killed, he told me he was on his way to his attorney's office to start divorce proceedings against her. And in answer to your second question, he came to see me because he wanted to know if I could help him with a problem he was having. He said he couldn't sleep at night because of the stress he'd been under trying to get approval to build the hotel and spa and then making the decision to divorce Marcy. He wanted to know if there was something he could do, like meditate or drink warm milk, or whatever."

"Do you think Marcy knew he was going to divorce her?"

"I have no idea. I don't even know if he went to his lawyer's office. Why?"

"Well, if she found out he was going to divorce her that might be a motive for the murder. Wonder when she left to go see her sister in Portland."

"Kelly, seems to me I remember you made a promise to Mike that you'd let him solve the crimes that occur around here and you wouldn't get involved in his cases."

"Yeah, Doc, you're right. I did promise him I'd stay out of his cases. Okay, I won't," she said, mentally crossing her fingers and wondering when Marcy and Brandon would return to Cedar Bay so she could talk to Marcy. "Speaking of which, it's time for us to go. Mike wanted to tell Brandon about the death of his father in person, so he drove over to Corvallis and didn't get any sleep last night. Rather imagine he'll want dinner as soon as I get home and then he'll crash. Thanks Doc, and I'm so glad your volunteering is working out for you.

"I need to start dinner, too. Liz asked me if I would give her some advice on a few of her clients and I asked her to come out here for dinner. Thought it would be easier to talk here rather than in the office, plus it saves me from having to drive back to town."

"Doc, you asked Liz out here for dinner? That's a first. At least I think that's a first. Is there more I should know about this relationship?"

"Kelly, you're starting to wear too darn many hats. Coffee shop owner, unlicensed crime solver, and now matchmaker. Stick to wearing the first hat and let go of the other two. If there's anything you need to know, I'll be sure and tell you, but only if and when I feel like it."

"I'm counting on it, Doc," she said, grinning. She opened the door and started to walk out. "Come on, Rebel. Time to go home."

Rebel stood where he was and looked up at Doc expectantly, at least that's the way it looked to Doc and Kelly who exchanged amused looks. Neither one was sure if a dog could look expectantly, but if it could, that was the expression Rebel wore.

"All right, Rebel. I almost forgot your treat. Come on."

Rebel pranced into the kitchen and stood next to Doc. Kelly waited while Doc cut several pieces of filet mignon into bite size pieces and fed them to Rebel. When Rebel was finished eating he walked over to where Kelly was waiting and followed her out to her minivan. Doc walked along with them and opened the door on the minivan for her.

"Kelly, I'd swear that dog wasn't going to leave until he got his treat and he knows I always give him filet mignon pieces. That big guy is almost human."

"I know. He even scares me at times. See you tomorrow."

CHAPTER SIX

"Hey, Mike. I'm home," Kelly said as she walked into the great room that overlooked the bay. Mike rose from the chair he'd been sitting in and strode over to her, enveloping her in a big hug and giving her a kiss.

"Where have you been? I've been expecting you for the last couple of hours. Either you've been cooking a lot at the coffee shop or you've been running errands."

"Don't know if it would qualify as running errands, but first of all I went out to the reservation. Chief Many Trees asked me to bring him some cookies and leftover caramel rolls, if there were any, for a tribal council meeting they're holding tonight. I had a long talk with him and it was quite interesting. Don't worry, Mike, I'm not getting involved in this case, although what he told me might have some bearing on your investigation." She related to him the conversation she had with Chief Many Trees.

"Kelly, that's very interesting, but it still doesn't mean that someone from the reservation wasn't the killer. He or she could have easily gotten a gun and killed Jeff. The fact that guns aren't allowed on the reservation only means just that. Someone could hide a gun anywhere, on or off the reservation."

"I know, Mike, but I would think that alone would keep a lot of people from buying one and using it."

"If threatening to kick someone out of the tribe is a deterrent to having easy access to guns, I'm all for it. The hard truth of the matter is that it's very easy for anyone to get a gun and keep it hidden. Look at all the people you read about carrying concealed weapons that don't have a permit. Anyway, I want to tell you about my conversation with Lem Bates. He's the lawyer in town."

"Mike, I know who Lem is. I've known him forever. We went to school together. He's the only lawyer in town, so he knows everybody and pretty much everything about everybody. Anyway, go on."

"Yeah, I forget sometimes that your roots run a lot deeper here in Cedar Bay than mine. I've been sitting here for an hour or so trying to figure out what to do with this information. Evidently Jeff was pretty sure Marcy was having an affair with Gabe Lewis, you know, the lumber baron who lives up in Sunset Bay."

"Mike, I can't believe you learned today that Marcy was having an affair, because, believe it or not, I found out the same thing just an hour or so ago. I'll tell you how I found out when you finish."

"Kelly, what Lem told me was essentially attorney-client privileged information, but Lem said that since Jeff was dead, it really didn't matter anymore, so he was free to tell me why Jeff had come to see him."

"Yep. That's exactly what I was told."

"Look, we're getting nowhere really fast. How about you be quiet and listen to me and then I'll be quiet and listen to you. Fair enough?"

"Deal."

"Okay. Jeff was so sure Marcy was having an affair with Gabe that he started divorce proceedings against her. In the court papers Lem prepared and filed with the court, it specified that the ranch was Jeff's sole and separate property. He'd inherited part of the property from his parents and the rest of the acreage he bought at a BLM auction. He used his inheritance from his parents to buy the BLM property. If you remember, when I did a background search on him when he was a suspect in Amber's murder, I found out that the ranch was solely in his name. Here's the interesting part. Jeff took out a life insurance policy on himself in the amount of three million dollars several years ago. He wanted to make sure that if something ever happened to him, Brandon would have enough money to go to both college and graduate school. He told Lem he wasn't going to change anything on the insurance policy. He wanted Marcy to stay on as the primary beneficiary so she would have money to pay for Brandon's education. He said that although Marcy was almost assuredly having an affair with Gabe, she was still a very good mother."

"Wow! Between the divorce and the life insurance policy, she certainly had a motive, actually a couple, for killing him."

"Well, there's more. She didn't know that the ranch and everything in it was in Jeff's name alone and would be awarded exclusively to him if there was a divorce. From what Lem said, she was never interested in the business side of things. She thought the ranch was in both of their names. Lem personally served her with the divorce papers and according to him, when she read them she went nuts. She couldn't believe that she would be almost penniless after the divorce. He said she was shocked Jeff was divorcing her. She kept saying that if something happened to Jeff she wouldn't have any money to keep Brandon in school. Lem told her that even though Jeff was divorcing her, he had insisted on keeping her on as the primary beneficiary on his life insurance policy in order to provide a fund to pay for Brandon's education. He also told her the policy amount was three million dollars and with that amount, she would have more than enough money to keep Brandon in school. He told her she would be entitled to spousal support because of the longevity of the marriage, but if she remarried, it would end."

"Mike, when did Lem serve her with the divorce papers?"

"From your question, you're probably thinking the same thing I am. She was served in the afternoon on the day Jeff was murdered."

Kelly was quiet for several minutes while she began to prepare dinner. "Mike, after I took the things out to the chief at the reservation, I went to see Doc. I was curious how he was doing at the clinic and his ranch was on the way home. Interestingly enough, Jeff had talked to Doc at the clinic about divorcing Marcy for the same reason Lem told you, namely, she was having an affair with Gabe Lewis. He knew Doc wasn't a psychologist, but he was hoping Doc could give him some advice about problems he was having with sleeping. He said between getting approval for the hotel and spa and making the difficult decision to divorce Marcy, he hadn't had a good night's sleep in months. He told Doc he didn't want to meet with Liz because they'd known each other a long time. He didn't feel she could be objective about his situation."

"Well, whether she was having an affair with him or not, Jeff was sure enough about it to make the decision to divorce her. You've got a good sense of things and people. Think Marcy did it?"

"I don't know. If she was found guilty of killing Jeff, it would mean both of Brandon's parents would be gone. His mother would be in prison for life for the murder of his father. That, on top of the recent murder of his girlfriend, Amber, might be too much for him. Whatever else people say about Marcy, she's a very good mother and I'm not sure she would do anything to hurt Brandon. For that reason alone, I have a hard time thinking it's her, but I could be wrong."

"Kelly, my brain is too tired from lack of sleep for me to even think clearly right now. How about we finish dinner and then I can go to bed? Hopefully, the answer will come to me when I wake up tomorrow, but I have a feeling that's not going to happen."

"Well, I'll give you something lighter to think about. Liz, the psychologist in town who owns the clinic where Doc is donating his time, is going out to Doc's home for dinner tonight. I think that's a little unusual, don't you?"

"You know him a lot better than I do, but from what you've told me, he's kind of a loner. I've never heard of anyone being asked to his ranch. You've been out there a couple of times, but I don't think you were invited. Are you inferring that maybe there's a possibility of some romance in the air?"

"Well, I don't know. He was rather evasive when I asked him, but I hope there is something going on between the two of them. Both of them are nice people who deserve some happiness. You know Doc's situation and that certainly hasn't been a happy one. Liz is kind of a Mother Earth figure. You just feel better when you're around her. No wonder she's such a successful psychologist. I don't think her life has been all that happy either, although she clearly enjoys being a psychologist. I remember Liz telling me she was briefly married when she was in her early twenties, but I've never heard of her seeing anyone else and she's got to be in her mid-40's now. She lived in Portland for several years, and then came back here to be with her parents before they passed away."

"Sounds to me like she'd be perfect for him," Mike said. They're both in the medical field and she's a little younger than he is. She doesn't have any children, does she?"

"No. One time we were talking about children because she counsels several at the clinic and that's when she made the statement that although she'd been married briefly, she'd never had children. I think I told you that Doc has two sons, but when he was tried for manslaughter in Southern California and his wife left him, she took the children and he's never seen them since. I wonder if Doc has told Liz about his past. Don't you think she'd be curious why he wasn't practicing medicine? Wouldn't it be wonderful if Liz and Doc got together and his sons reconciled with him? I think he said they were teenagers when the marriage broke up, so they might even be in college by now."

"Well, sweetheart, knowing you, I'm sure you'll have the answers to all of those question in a few days. I like your rationale for what you do. I think you told me once that you're not prying, you're simply gathering information."

Kelly wadded up the dishtowel she had in her hand and threw it at him. "Careful, Sheriff Mike, next time it could be a knife and even though you weren't very pleased with me, you know I helped you solve Amber's murder."

"So you did, Kelly, so you did. And I'm really happy that you promised me that you would never get involved in any of my cases again, right?" he asked with a stern look on his face.

"That's right," she said, mentally crossing her fingers. "I promised, didn't I?"

CHAPTER SEVEN

Kelly looked out from the kitchen of Kelly's Koffee Shop and said, "Roxie, looks like we've got a bit of a lull in the action here at the moment. I'm going to make a bank run. I won't be gone long."

"No problem, Kelly. Seems like a good time to go. See you in a few minutes."

Kelly walked the two blocks to the First Federal Bank. As she was reaching to open the door, it was suddenly pushed open from the inside and she was thrown a couple of steps back. Two people rushed out the door. It was Marcy Black and a man Kelly couldn't identify. She overheard him say, "Don't worry, Marcy. Brandon and I will make sure you have enough money to live on." The man continued to talk, but his words were lost as they hurried over to a late model silver-colored car. Kelly watched as the man opened the door for Marcy and then got in the car and rapidly drove away.

Wonder who that is. I thought I knew everyone for miles around.

She opened the door of the bank again and walked over to Patti, the teller. "Kelly, I saw what happened. They almost knocked you down. Are you all right?"

"I'm fine. I recognized Marcy Black, but I can't place the man that was with her. They both seemed pretty angry."

"Yeah, I probably shouldn't tell you this, but I've never seen anything like it. Mrs. Black had a key to a safe deposit box and wanted to open it up. I checked and she was authorized to do that. She wanted the man who was with her to come into the vault with us, so I had him sign the entry log we keep where the names of everyone who enters the vault are recorded. We both put our keys in and opened the box. She started to look in it, but the man, his name is Gabe Lewis, according to the entry log, pushed her aside, grabbed what looked like a will, and quickly read it. He almost threw it at Mrs. Black and said, 'He cut you out of his will. Everything goes to Brandon.'"

"Wow! How did she take it?"

"Not well, she was furious. He told Mrs. Black to stay calm and they'd talk about it later, then they left, taking the will with them. Kelly, I really shouldn't have told you any of this. Please don't tell anyone else what I just said."

"Not to worry. I promise I won't tell anyone," she said, mentally crossing her fingers and thinking that Mike needed to know about this. It seemed to Kelly that it could be very important to his investigation.

"Here's my deposit, Patti. I better get back to the coffee shop before Roxie decides to quit because I left her alone," she said, handing the teller a leather pouch containing the receipts from the coffee shop for the last couple of days. Patti handed the deposit slip to her and Kelly hurried back to the coffee shop.

*****

"Looks like you handled everything just fine, Roxie," Kelly said. "Thanks."

"No problem. Oh, by the way, Doc called and said he wanted to talk to you when he comes in at noon today."

"Any idea what's up with him? That's kind of unusual."

"Nope, that's all he said. I told him I'd give you the message when you got back from the bank."

"Okay, I'll keep an eye out for him."

Promptly at noon, just as he did every Monday through Friday, Doc opened the coffee shop door and walked in. Rebel stood up and walked over to him, hoping for a filet mignon treat, or at the very least, an ear scratch.

"Sorry, boy, don't have any treats with me, but I can scratch those ears for a minute," Doc said, bending down while Rebel's wagging tail became a blur.

"Hi, Doc," Kelly said as she walked over to him. "Understand you wanted to talk to me."

"Yeah. Mind if we go in the storeroom for a couple of minutes? I'd just as soon our talk was a little more private than out here where everyone can hear us."

"Sure, follow me."

She closed the storeroom door. "Doc, this is totally unlike you. What's up?"

"Well, I just had a conversation with Bonnie Davis. She came to see me because she'd heard I was working with people who were having problems with substance abuse. Evidently her husband drinks a couple of six packs of beer every night."

"Wait a minute, Doc, should you be telling me this? To my knowledge she's not dead and you said the only reason you could tell me about Jeff Black was because he was dead. Don't you have an ethical obligation to someone you're counseling?"

"That's true, Kelly, but Bonnie told me this in the waiting room of the clinic. We weren't in my office and a room full of people also heard her tell me."

"Okay, Doc. Just didn't want you to get in trouble for telling me something you shouldn't."

"Thanks, I appreciate it. We both know I've had enough trouble with at least one State Medical Board. I sure don't want any more problems in that area. As a counselor, I feel that what people tell me is privileged information and I would never breach a confidence, but this was not one of those times."

"Okay, what did she say?"

"We talked about her husband and then she said she'd been away from home a lot in the last few months, trying to put a stop to the hotel and spa that Jeff Black was going to build on his property out at Jade Cove. She said it would damage the environment and nothing that big should be built that close to the ocean and the steep cliff at Jade Cove. Then she started talking about the spotted owls and how several had been seen in the Jade Cove area. She was jumping all over the place, from one topic to another, but everything she talked about was related to the environment. She told me the spotted owl was on the endangered species list and that its habitat would be harmed if anything like the hotel and spa were built on the Black's property. She actually worked herself up to what I would almost consider a frenzy. She's really passionate about it. I wanted to talk to you and see if you know her. That's my first experience being around her."

"You can't live in a city this size and not know Bonnie Davis," Kelly said. Some people think she's a real nut case. I don't think there's ever been a County Board of Supervisors meeting or a City Council meeting where she didn't get up and speak out about something in the environment that was going to be harmed by whatever was being proposed. I think she's the president of something called the Wildlife Advocates. She travels all around the state and speaks to groups whenever some proposed development threatens the environment. I've heard that her husband drinks too much and I think there are a lot of people who feel that's the only way he can stay married to her."

"To tell you the truth, I had the same feeling. I just wanted to pick your brain since you know everyone around here and see if this is something I may want to avoid getting involved with."

"I guess that's a decision you'll have to make on your own. Doc, a thought just occurred to me. Did she say anything else about Jeff Black?"

"Yes, I was concentrating more on what she was saying about her husband, but she did make the statement that she'd been trying to keep Jeff Black from building on his property because of the spotted owls. She said it was a good thing he was dead, that maybe now the owls in that area could be saved. Now that I think about it, she's probably someone who might have had a reason to kill him."

There was a knock on the storeroom door. "Come in," Kelly said.

"Kelly, I don't know where they're comin' from, but I need you up front. There are more people here than I can handle."

"Be there in a sec, Roxie," Kelly said as Roxie closed the door.

"Doc, thanks for telling me. On second thought, I'd stay away from her if I were you. Her husband's been drinking excessively for as long as I can remember, and even if he stopped, it probably wouldn't keep her from traveling and speaking out about the environment. She's really fanatical about it. I don't think I've ever heard her talk about anything else. I'll see what else I can find out about her because based on what you just told me, she very well might be a suspect in the Jeff Black murder."

"Kelly, let me give you some advice. You'd be better off telling Mike and letting him see what he can find out. Remember, this is his case."

"You're right, Doc. I'll tell Mike and I promise you I'll stay out of it," she said, crossing her fingers and wondering if this was something she was going to have to explain to St. Peter when she got to the Pearly Gates or if she could get a pass if she confessed her habit of telling "white lies" to Father Brown the next time she went to church.

CHAPTER EIGHT

Kelly locked the coffee shop door and stood for a moment, looking out at the bay.

It's so tranquil it's hard to believe that two murders have occurred in this little town in a matter of months. I guess it's like everything else. No matter how calm and serene it seems on the surface, there's always something going on underneath it, just like the bay. Doesn't look like anything much even lives in the bay, but dive down and it's full of fish, abalone, crabs, kelp, and every other form of aquatic life.

She and Rebel got in her minivan and pulled out of the parking lot. *I know I promised Mike I wouldn't get involved in the Jeff Black murder case, but this isn't really getting involved. I just want to talk to Bonnie about the spotted owls.* She heard a voice in the back of her head saying, *"Sure you do."* She ignored it.

She parked her minivan in front of the Davis' house. "Stay, boy. I won't be long," she said to Rebel who promptly stood up in the passenger seat, insuring that no one would be entering the minivan until Kelly returned.

Even though it was November, someone in the Davis household had carefully tended the plants in the numerous pots leading up to the front porch. Vivid green ivy grew across the front of the freshly painted white house. Crisp green and white checkered curtains were pulled back in the front windows which looked out at the bay. It was a very warm and inviting home. Kelly knocked on the front door and admired the colorful wreath of fall leaves which surrounded the peephole.

In a moment the door was opened by Jack Davis. "Can I help you?" he asked.

"Jack, it's Kelly Conner. Remember me? You've come to my coffee shop several times, but I haven't seen you there recently. I stopped by to see if Bonnie was available. I want to ask her some questions about the spotted owls and I understand she's an expert on the subject.

"Sorry, Kelly, I didn't recognize you. Please, come in. She's an expert on the spotted owls, all right. I'll get her."

He returned a few minutes later followed by a grey-haired woman who wore Birkenstock sandals, a long flowing skirt, and a heavy knit sweater. Her hair was pulled into a conservative bun at the nape of her neck. She wore no make-up, not even lipstick. Looking at her, Kelly was reminded of the hippies who had come through Cedar Bay on their way to San Francisco in the late '60s and early '70s. The only thing missing from Bonnie's dated clothing was a tie-dye patterned T-shirt. There were a few pictures of some hippies on the walls in the coffee shop along with other pictures of the changes that had occurred in Cedar Bay over the years. Bonnie looked very much like the people in those photos from several decades ago. As she looked at her, Kelly thought that Bonnie's time had come and gone. There was nothing contemporary about her looks or clothing.

"Hi, Bonnie, I haven't seen you for a long time. If you have a minute, I'd like to talk to you."

"Kelly, it's good to see you. I have to leave fairly soon for a meeting in Sunset Bay, but I have a little time. What can I do for you?"

"Well, a tourist was in the coffee shop the other day asking if I knew where any nesting sites for spotted owls were located. Evidently he's a fairly new member of the Audubon Society and wanted to take a photograph of one while he was visiting in Oregon so he could show it to his bird-watching group when he got back to Kansas. I told him I didn't know a thing about them. After he left I started thinking about my conversation with him, and since we get so many tourists at the coffee shop, I figured I probably should know something about them. I understand they're on the endangered species list, but that's about all I know. I mentioned to a friend that I was interested in learning more about spotted owls and he said you were an expert on the subject. I happened to be in the area so I thought I'd stop by and see if you were home and could spare me a moment."

"Please, have a seat. Jack, would you get us some coffee?" she asked, turning towards her husband. A few minutes later he returned with mugs for each of them.

"Here you are. I'd join you, but I have to meet my hunting pal Fred out at the rifle range. When I was deer hunting I noticed that my favorite hunting rifle was missing the target by a couple of inches, so I'm going to test it out at the range. I'm pretty sure the telescopic sight just needs a little fine tuning. When those cross-hairs on the scope are properly adjusted, just about anybody could hit smack dab in the middle of a half dollar at two hundred yards. That's why it's my favorite. Don't get many chances to take a shot at a big buck and I don't want to miss an opportunity because the sights on my rifle are not properly adjusted. Glad it's only the one rifle I'm having trouble with because if I had to test fire all five of my rifles I'd be out at the range all day. See you later." They heard the screen door close behind him as he walked out towards the garage.

Bonnie looked at Kelly with a smile on her face and said, "It's such a big subject I really don't know where to begin. You probably want an overview. Well, the spotted owls live in old-growth forests, so there are a lot of them around here. You're correct in that it is an endangered species. I don't know if you're aware of it, but they've been seen on Jeff Black's property. The main threat to the spotted owls is the loss of their habitat. If Jeff's land is cleared for that hotel and spa he wanted to build, that would qualify as habitat loss.

"I've spoken at a number of meetings about it. In fact, I even traveled to Washington D.C. to meet with our Senators and Congressmen about it. I wasn't able to see them, but I did have meetings with their staffs. They told me that unless there were photographs or hard evidence of a spotted owl on the Black property, there was nothing they could do. I tried my darnedest, but I couldn't get a picture of one on his property."

Bonnie stopped for a moment and took a sip of her coffee. "Not many people know that there's an old dilapidated shack on that strip of Bureau of Land Management property on the north side of Jade Cove. I found it years ago when I was bird-watching in that area. Nobody's ever in that shack, just mice and birds. The windows were broken out before I ever went there and there's a big hole in the roof. When I was there many years ago I remembered that even though it's not on Jeff Black's property, you can see the shack he used as an office as well as his ranch house from the vantage point of the abandoned shack. I thought it would be a good idea for me to go hide out in the old shack and see if I could get a photo of a spotted owl on his property."

"Can anyone get on the BLM property?" Kelly asked. "I kind of remember seeing a "No Trespassing" sign on it."

"Yeah, well, there may be. Anyway, I had a telephoto lens on my camera that's also equipped with an infrared attachment so I can take photos at night. Believe me, if an owl had come, I was ready, but I didn't see anything. It was a full moon when I was there. I stayed awake at night watching for an owl and slept during the day. I was out there for two days and nights. Unfortunately, I couldn't get the proof I needed and the hotel and spa were approved. Best thing that ever happened to the spotted owls was when Jeff Black was killed. Sure hope whoever's going to take over that land now that he's dead won't try to build on it. I have some people coming in a couple of days who are really good bird watchers. They can see birds that no one else can and I'm hoping they can get a picture of one on his property. I understand that whoever inherits the property won't have to get approval again to build a hotel and spa, but if I can get a photograph of a spotted owl on that property, I can probably get the Oregon Fish and Wildlife Department to back me up and stop any future construction."

"Wow! I had no idea that if something like the spotted owl is on the endangered species list, a loss of its habitat might stop something from being built," Kelly said. "I'll bet a lot of people haven't been very happy when that happened."

"I look at it this way. Someone has to look out for our wild animals and creatures. They can't speak for themselves. I consider it to be my life's work to see what I can do to help them. Make no mistake, Kelly, that hotel and spa will never be built on that property."

Kelly stood up. "Thanks, Bonnie. I've taken up enough of your time and you mentioned you had a meeting you had to get to. I really appreciate you sharing all this information with me."

Bonnie walked her to the door. "I know you can't do anything about that property, but I hope you understand just how critical it is to the spotted owls. How would you like it if someone threatened to tear down your home and you couldn't speak up?"

Kelly paused for a moment and looked at her. "I wouldn't like it, Bonnie. I wouldn't like it at all."

As soon as Rebel saw Kelly approaching the minivan, he got in the back seat and laid down, his job of watching and waiting for her safe return over for the moment. "Thanks, boy. Wow, Bonnie may be a nut case, but she sure makes a pretty good argument for protecting the spotted owls. Who knew? Not me. Time to go home, big guy."

Bonnie stood at the window watching Kelly get into her van. When she saw Kelly drive around the corner, Bonnie walked up the stairs and went into her bedroom. She slid her closet door open and reached behind a heavy coat hanging at the far end of it. She removed a cloth bag from a hanger and unzipped it.

"It's okay, Big Eyes," Bonnie said." No one will ever find you. You know you'll always be safe with me because I love you more than anything in the world." She stroked the stuffed spotted owl and then put her arms around it's nearly one and a half foot tall body. "That mean old Jeff Black is dead and I'm glad. He was the only one who could hurt us. I told you about how he found me out at the old shack next to his property. He saw me shoot you several years ago and he threatened to tell everyone that I killed a spotted owl. He even took a photograph of me with you. He wanted to know why I'd done it. I told him how I loved spotted owls and I had to have one just for myself. He was going to tell everyone about how I killed you, but they would never be able to understand why I did it. I don't want to share you with anyone. I just wanted my own spotted owl. Don't worry, Big Eyes, our secret is safe now that Jeff's dead. I love you."

CHAPTER NINE

Kelly walked into the house and looked out the great room window where the light from the setting sun was spreading fingers of fading sunlight onto the smooth surface of the bay. No matter how many evenings she watched the sun set across Cedar Bay, it never failed to thrill her. The ringing of her cell phone broke her moment of reverie.

She looked at the monitor and answered it. "Hi, Mike. I kind of expected to see you when I got home. Something come up?"

"Yeah, a bunch of things. I've got a meeting with the coroner in a few minutes regarding Jeff's death. Marcy's back in town and I made an appointment to see her later on tonight. I was hoping to talk to Brandon, but she told me he's gone back to school. He and Marcy decided not to have a funeral for Jeff. He was cremated and Brandon said he'd prefer to remember his father the way he was the last time he saw Jeff. It's kind of a grey area because although Marcy had been served with the divorce papers, they weren't divorced, so according to the law, she still has the right to make the decision as what to do with Jeff's remains. Think it was gracious of her to bow to Brandon's wishes."

"Well, if she hadn't been served with the papers, I think she would have loved to have played the part of the grieving widow, but given the fact that Jeff cut her out of his will and was in the process of divorcing her, I think she made the right decision. When people find out about those two things, she'd look pretty ridiculous…"

Mike interrupted her. "Wait a minute. What are you talking about? What will?"

She told him what Patti, the teller at the bank, had told her. "Kelly, why would she tell you that? That's pretty confidential information."

"Mike, she and I grew up together. I've known her all my life, plus I think she still resents Marcy. Patti and Jeff were seeing each other before he met Marcy while he was in Portland on a business trip. I remember it was quite the talk of the town. Wealthy man goes to Portland and comes back with a prospective bride. Patti told me he broke it to her over the phone. It happened really fast and no one in town could believe it. Looks like Marcy knew a good thing when she saw it."

"Kelly, you promised me you wouldn't do anything on this case. You're skating on very thin ice here."

"Mike, I didn't ask her about the will. She volunteered the information. You know I'd never break a promise to you," she said, mentally crossing her fingers.

"Well, remember what you just said the next time you're tempted to 'help me' and believe me, I use the term loosely. I suppose that explains why Lem called earlier. When I saw him yesterday, he mentioned that Jeff's will was in his safe deposit box. He probably read the file copy of Jeff's will that he kept in his office and after he read it, called me. That gives Marcy an even stronger motive to kill Jeff. Anger over him divorcing her, leaving her out of his will, and finding out she was the beneficiary of a three million dollar life insurance policy."

"I agree, Mike, but don't forget Marcy just found out today that Jeff left her out of his will. If you consider her a prime suspect, you have to remember that she didn't know she had been cut out of his will when he was murdered. I would think she'd want to get a good divorce attorney instead and hope she could get some of the ranch property. That would be worth far more than the three million dollars in insurance money she'd get if he was dead."

"That's true, but maybe it was a question of the old saying, 'a bird in the hand is worth more than two in the bush,' in other words, she could always kill him if she didn't get part of the ranch property in the divorce. She's not dumb. Marcy would probably figure that Jeff would keep her on as the primary beneficiary of the policy until Brandon finished college, so she knew she had some time. Yes, she had a motive, but I think she might have even had more of a motive to see that he lived. Plus, I'm sure she would have gotten some alimony from Jeff, and if he died, she'd lose it."

"Mike, a thought just occurred to me. Do you think Brandon knew that according to the terms of Jeff's will, he was going to inherit everything? If he did, that certainly provides a motive for Brandon to be the killer. You know, kill Jeff and he gets the ranch now rather than years from now when Jeff dies from natural causes."

There was quiet on the other end of the phone while Mike thought about what Kelly had just said. Finally, he answered her, "Yes, that would provide a motive and no, I don't know if Brandon knew about the will. With Jeff dead, I'm not sure we'll ever know. I'm reluctant to consider that Brandon could have done it because I remember how close and supportive Brandon was to Jeff when the fire destroyed his property. Remember, after I arrested Jeff for growing marijuana on his property, and he was in the county jail for a couple of days trying to make bail, Brandon was the one who stuck by his dad. Marcy abandoned him and left for Portland to be with her sister and threatened to divorce him. She made Brandon go to Portland with her, but when he came back to Cedar Bay to deliver the valedictorian speech at his high school graduation, he stayed at the ranch house with Jeff. It was a few more weeks before Marcy returned. No, I would have a real hard time thinking that Brandon killed his father."

"Well, Sheriff Mike, I have another person in mind for you. Does the name Bonnie Davis ring a bell with you?"

"No, it doesn't just sound like a ringing bell when her name is mentioned, it's more like a loud abrasive gong. I can't tell you how many times I've listened to her speak at various events, usually about the spotted owls. Why do you ask?"

"I had a long talk with her today. A tourist was at the coffee shop a few weeks ago and asked where he could find spotted owls. He said he wanted to take a picture of one and show it to his Audubon Society group back in Kansas. I didn't know a thing about them, so I stopped by her house and asked if she would tell me about the spotted owls," Kelly said as she walked into the nearby bathroom and looked in the mirror to see if her nose had grown as long as Pinocchio's had grown for lying.

"Here's the thing," she continued, "Bonnie fought long and hard to try and stop the construction of the hotel and spa on Jeff's property. She told me she was glad Jeff was dead because maybe it meant that now the hotel and spa wouldn't be built. She said she considered herself to be a voice for the spotted owls. I think she meant it. She may be a nut case, but she also had a motive for killing Jeff."

"Well, that may be so, but I'd have a tough time believing Bonnie's a killer," Mike said.

"Here's one more tidbit of information about Bonnie that you might find interesting. When I was at her house, her husband Jack was there when I arrived and he said he had to leave to go to the rifle range. Seems he was having trouble with the telescopic sight on one of his hunting rifles and was going to the range and test it. In passing he mentioned that he owns five rifles. That means Bonnie would have easy access to Jack's rifles if she wanted to kill Jeff. Jack also said that with the telescopic sight on his rifle, it was easy to hit a target anywhere from one hundred to two hundred yards. Yeah, I know Bonnie is outspoken in her opposition to guns and supports a ban on the sale of guns, but nevertheless, the old saying, 'Where there's a will, there's a way' might apply to Bonnie. Jack's rifle could have very easily provided the 'way' for Bonnie to kill Jeff," Kelly said.

"I'd forgotten how opposed Bonnie was to that project, probably because she's been opposed to so many projects over the years. Yes, she would have a motive. I'll put her on my list of possible suspects. So, let's see, at the moment we have Marcy, someone from the tribe, Brandon, and now Bonnie. They're all as different as night and day, and yet, I would have to say that each one of them definitely had a motive for murdering Jeff. Gotta go, babe, don't want to be late for my meeting. Go to bed. I'll probably get home past your bedtime. See you in the morning and sleep well. I love you."

"Love you too."

I really don't know much about Gabe Lewis other than he's from old lumber money and there's plenty of it. Think I'll spend a few minutes and see what Google turns up about him. An hour and a half later she pushed her chair back from the computer and rubbed her eyes.

Well, this is interesting. He's a lumber baron who also owns the largest lumber mill on the west coast and although he used to be quite wealthy, lately he's been having some serious financial problems. According to what I read, he's quite an outdoor sportsman and belongs to several exclusive hunting clubs.

His wife owns a business called Lewis Kennels. She breeds and sells hunting dogs. Evidently people pay a lot of money for the dogs and her clients are located all over the country. She specializes in chocolate labs, but also breeds yellow labs. One article mentioned that although he had once been engaged to a woman named Marcy Jordan from Portland, he broke the engagement and married a woman whose family founded Sunset Bay during the last century.

I wonder if Marcy's maiden name was Jordan. Might fit. Her sister lives in Portland and I think that's where she grew up. I remember Jeff going there on business and coming back with his prospective bride, Marcy. Don't know what any of this means, but it might come in handy. What if Marcy and Gabe were an item at one time and then recently reconnected? Maybe they wanted to get married and Gabe killed Jeff. Other than that, I can't figure out any other reason Gabe would have for killing Jeff. Think Jeff had more of a reason to kill Gabe than the other way around. This is too much information for me to process. I'm on overload. Time for bed.

"Come on, Rebel, let's wind it up for tonight," she said, opening the back door for him. "I need to eat something and then I'm going to fall into bed. Tomorrow will come way too soon and my brain is so tired from absorbing everything that's happened today, I need to shut it off for awhile."

CHAPTER TEN

The next morning when Kelly woke up she looked over at Mike who was sleeping peacefully next to her and thought, *I really love this man. I'm so glad he asked me to marry him.* She quietly reached for the alarm and turned it off, not wanting it to wake him.

I wonder what time he made it home last night. I never even heard him get into bed. I'm really curious what the coroner and Marcy had to say. Well, from the looks of him, it will have to wait. He's out like a light.

She motioned for Rebel to follow her. She opened the back door for him, fed him, made a quick cup of coffee, and got dressed. Fifteen minutes later she and Rebel were in the van on the way to the coffee shop.

I am so looking forward to this weekend. I could use a break. Whenever something happens in Cedar Bay, it seems everyone has to come to the coffee shop to talk about it. I'm not complaining because the more people that come in, the better the coffee shop does financially, but I really get tired of having to talk all the time. I know Mike would never believe that, but it's true. I'd like to sleep in and do nothing. Maybe I'll even go out to Scott's retreat center and take a yoga and meditation class. That always seems to relax me and I haven't been there in quite awhile.

Just like they had the previous day, the townspeople congregated at Kelly's Koffee Shop, hoping that someone had something new to share about Jeff Black's murder. Kelly and Roxie were busy from the moment the first customer arrived.

Slightly before noon, Kelly heard a welcoming woof coming from Rebel and looked up as Mike came through the door. He put his Stetson hat on the hat rack and reached down to scratch Rebel's ears. "Morning, sweetheart," he said, looking up at Kelly. "What's the special today? I slept like a baby and I'm starving."

"Well since it's almost noon, how about some of those special baked beans with hamburger you've always liked, you know the ones called Calico Bean Bake? I can fix you a great chicken salad sandwich that would go well with them."

"You don't need to go any farther. I'd like an extra-large serving if you don't mind. You can arrange for that, can't you? Seems to me I should get a perk for being engaged to the owner, don't you think?" he asked, winking at her. "I'd also like an iced tea."

"No problem, since you're absolutely my favorite sheriff. By the way, have you been giving Rebel special treats when I'm not around?"

"Nope. You asked me not to, so I haven't. Why do you ask?"

"Well, look where he is, under the table at your feet. He doesn't do that for anyone else who comes in here. He's always on his bed by the cash register or back in the kitchen with me, not under a table, which makes me think you're slipping him things when I'm not looking."

"Kelly, Kelly, I'm shocked that you'd think that. Why, since you never tell fibs to me, how can you even suggest that I might be telling you a fib?" Mike asked with a wide-eyed innocent looking expression on his face.

She rolled her eyes at him and went into the kitchen to get his order and waited for Rebel to follow her into the kitchen. He didn't.

Now I'm sure of it. Mike's got to be feeding him when I'm not looking. I'm probably going to lose him to Mike. Just might have to get a puppy for me. That'll show Mike. A wedding present from me to me.

She set the iced tea and a heaping plate of the Calico Bean Bake along with a large chicken salad sandwich in front of him and sat down at the table. "Mike, when you come up for air, I'd like to hear what happened last night."

He was silent for a few minutes, enjoying the beans and sandwich. "Okay, my stomach has stopped screaming, so I guess I can take a break. It was an interesting evening. The coroner placed Jeff's death at about 4:30 p.m. He told me Jeff died from a gunshot wound which we already knew. What we didn't know was that he was shot with a 30-30 hunting rifle. There was no gunpowder residue on his body, so the shot must have been taken from quite a distance. That was the first interesting thing."

"Wow! I would think that would help you narrow down the list of suspects. Not many people around here own a high-powered hunting rifle."

"It doesn't really help me. It could have been someone who was hunting where they shouldn't have been, thought they saw a deer, and shot Jeff instead. I'll probably never find them if that's the case."

"Yeah, that's true. What was the other interesting thing?"

"Well, I had a long talk with Marcy. She's not happy that everything was in Jeff's name, but since their divorce wasn't finalized and she was on a couple of his bank accounts, she still has access to some of his funds. Brandon told her she could live in the house as long as she wanted to and since he was named as the executor of Jeff's will, he also told her he wouldn't close the accounts or take away her credit cards. Even though she won't inherit anything from Jeff, she still has access to most of what she had while he was alive. She was actually quite calm, at least not angry like you'd described her when you saw her at the bank a few hours earlier."

"So she's going to stay in the house for now. Any talk about whether the hotel and spa are going to be built?"

"We didn't talk about it specifically, but if she's going to stay in the house that would mean it isn't going to be razed for the construction project any time soon. I'm assuming that it's not going to be built right now. I did get a call from Lem last night. He told me he agreed to help Brandon. Kid just can't do everything that needs to be done and try and stay in school. Lem's got a lot of business sense and Jeff trusted him. I think he'll be a big help to Brandon. You may remember that even though Jeff was going to build the hotel and spa on his property, Lem was opposed to it. He thought a project of that size would result in too great a change to our sleepy little town. I imagine he would advise Brandon not to build the hotel and spa on the property. If Brandon needs money, he can always sell off part of the property or subdivide it. With its great location, it would be very desirable in the real estate market."

He looked around to see if anyone was listening to them and then leaned close across the table and quietly said, "She did tell me something quite interesting and also a little disturbing. It looks like there's another possible suspect."

"Get out! You've got to be kidding! Who?"

"A drug dealer from Mexico..."

Kelly interrupted him in a loud voice. "What are you talking about?"

"Kelly, keep your voice down." He looked around again to make sure no one was trying to overhear what he was saying. "Well, according to Marcy, she got a call yesterday from a man named Carlos Delgado. He said he had something to tell her about Jeff. She asked him what it was, but he said he could only tell her in person. He told her he was on his way to the ranch and would be there within the hour. Sure enough, he and another man arrived at the ranch about forty-five minutes after she got the call. She described Carlos as having a drooping mustache and a swarthy, scarred face with long greasy black hair. He had a large diamond stud earring in his left ear. Anyway, he told her he and Jeff were partners in the marijuana business. He said he had supplied Jeff with all of the money for the marijuana plants, the irrigation, and provided the workers for the marijuana farm Jeff was secretly operating on the back part of his property."

"Are you kidding me, Mike? This is pretty far-fetched. Jeff in cahoots with some Mexican drug cartel? Who would have thought?"

"Believe it or not, that's what she told me. Anyway, Carlos demanded that she pay him one and a half million dollars. He said he and Jeff had a deal that no matter what happened to the marijuana plants, whether they were confiscated by the narcs, whether the plants died from some disease, or whatever else, Jeff had to repay him the money he'd advanced to finance the construction and operation of the marijuana farm. When the marijuana farm burned down, Carlos had demanded that Jeff pay him, but Jeff refused. Now that Jeff was dead, he told Marcy she had to pay him what Jeff owed. Marcy told him she didn't have that kind of money and that Jeff had filed for divorce. Carlos told her the divorce had nothing to do with Jeff's promise and he wanted his money.

"She said Carlos motioned to the man with him and the man pulled out a switchblade knife and made a threatening gesture to Marcy. Carlos told her she better pay him or she'd have a scar on her face similar to the one the other man had on his face. Marcy told me the man had a horrible looking jagged scar that ran from his right eyebrow to below his chin. She said it was one of the most frightening things she'd ever seen. Then, without warning, the other man stepped behind Marcy, put his arm around her neck, and held the tip of his switchblade under her chin. She felt pain and looked down at the white blouse she was wearing. There was a drop of blood on it. The man released his hold on her and threw her to the ground. Carlos said he'd be back in a few days and she better have the money for him or Brandon might not be able to finish college because he'd be dead. Naturally she was panicked. She told Carlos she might be able to use the money from an insurance policy Jeff had taken out on his life since she was the primary beneficiary."

"Mike, this sounds like something out of a pulp fiction movie. Marcy isn't one of my favorite people, but I can't imagine the fear she must have felt when he threatened to harm her and kill Brandon."

"I'm sure she was terrified," Mike said. "She doesn't know what to do. She told me she has someone in mind that she thinks will loan her the money until she gets the proceeds from the life insurance policy."

"Wonder if she's thinking Gabe will loan her the money. From what I pulled up on the Internet last night about him, he seems to be having some serious financial problems of his own and I doubt he could loan her any money," Kelly said.

"That I don't know. I told Marcy to call me immediately if Carlos calls her again. Her sister's gone back to Portland so she's alone. I asked Marcy if she had a gun and she told me she did and that she wasn't afraid to use it. She said her father had belonged to a hunting club in Portland and always took her hunting with him. She said she was an excellent shot. Uh-oh, looks like your time with me is up."

Kelly looked over her shoulder and saw Roxie approaching. "Sorry to interrupt, Kelly, but I can't get out all of the orders that are ready to go in the kitchen. Need a little help, plus Zen Master Scott would like to talk to you."

"No problem. Mike and I were just finishing up. Mike, see you at home. Let's not make any plans for the weekend. Can you take a little time off from this case? We haven't spent much time together lately and I'd like to talk to you about our wedding. I know you're not terribly interested in the details, but I'd like to run some things by you."

"Sure," Mike said as he stood up. "Since we've been engaged a few months now, it's probably time to make this thing legal. Don't forget I asked your kids for permission to marry you. They may begin to wonder if I just wanted to move in with you, so yeah, let's plan on doing that this weekend."

As Kelly walked into the kitchen, Mike bent down and put his plate under the table so Rebel could lick the scraps off of it and whispered, "Don't tell her about this. It's our little secret." When Kelly opened the swinging doors of the kitchen a few minutes later, the plate was back on the table, clean as a whistle, Rebel was on his bed near the cash register, and Mike was getting into his sheriff's car. She may have suspected what had occurred between Mike and Rebel, but without proof, it was only just a suspicion.

*****

Zen Master Scott Monroe was the head of the White Cloud Retreat Center that was located about ten miles south of Cedar Bay. People came from all over the United States to take part in the retreats and residential programs he led as well as the workshops the center held. The beautiful large two story wood-faced house that was the center of the retreat area had been a lumber baron's in the last century and had a commanding view of the ocean from the hill where it sat. White clouds often settled around the hill and when Scott bought it from the lumber baron's heirs, he decided to name the center for the perpetually cloudy setting. He'd converted the large living room into a meditation room. Several other rooms in the main building and outlying buildings had been made into teaching and workshop areas. Twenty acres of vineyards surrounded the buildings and flourished in the cloudy and misty setting. The wine produced from them was a major source of income for the center. Zen students who stayed at the retreat center for the residential programs were required to work several hours a day in the vineyards.

Kelly had attended a couple of yoga workshops there over the years and had become friends with Scott, as he preferred to be called. He was a Zen Master whose feet were firmly planted in the here and now. The only time he wore the Zen robes was when he was leading something that required him to look official. He and Kelly had a shared interest in food and from time to time he stopped by the coffee shop to talk to her and occasionally bring her a bottle of wine that had been produced at the center. The center had a large wine tasting room which was open to the public and had developed quite a reputation for having excellent pinot noir wines.

The bearded burly man standing at the cash register dressed in jeans and a leather jacket bore no resemblance to what one would envision as a Zen Master, particularly one of the most revered contemporary Buddhists in the entire country. "Scott, it's so good to see you," Kelly said, kissing him on the cheek. How are things going out at the retreat center?"

"Busy, Kelly, really busy. There's been increasing interest all over the United States in meditation and every program we've recently offered has been filled to capacity. I'm even thinking of building two more dormitories to house all the people who want to come to the center. Don't get me wrong. I'm happy we're doing so well, but the people that come expect to spend some one-on-one time with the Zen Master and it really is impacting my time. I had a chance to escape today, so I dropped by to give you this bottle of wine. Consider it an early wedding present. I hear that you and Sheriff Mike are getting married and I couldn't be happier for you."

"Well, you'll definitely be at the top of the invitation list. If I wasn't Catholic, I'd want you to marry us, but right now I'm hoping Father Brown can perform the ceremony. I've known him so long he's kind of like family to me."

"I understand, but if for some reason that doesn't work out, keep me in mind. We're starting a week long Introduction to Zen program tomorrow and all the new students will be arriving in a few hours so I need to go back and get ready for them. Anyway, I hope you enjoy the wine and I'll see you at your wedding. Have you set a date yet?"

"No, funny you should ask. You just missed Mike and I was telling him we needed to discuss it this weekend. I'd like to get married around Valentine's Day. I know it's kind of trite, but I think it would be romantic."

"Well, if that's what you want to do, then just do it, and I don't think it's trite at all. I'm sure everyone else would agree with me. By the way, weddings can be pretty stressful. You know you're always welcome to come to the center and take a class or two. Hope to see you soon!"

"You're right. I've been thinking I need to do that. I always feel better when I take some classes. I just put it on my high priority list. Thanks again for stopping by and bringing the wine. I know we'll enjoy it and do me a favor, try not to work too hard. You're training all these people on how to deal with stress, but are you practicing what you preach?"

Scott threw back his head and laughed. "Isn't there some old saying about how the shoemaker's children had no shoes? I keep reminding myself that I can't stop my meditation practice, no matter how busy it gets. You haven't been out there in a year or so, but I have a pretty full staff. I've got seven monks and five nuns who assist me. Matter of fact, I even talked my brother into moving to the center from where he lives back East and helping me out. He's teaching some classes on stress reduction and yoga. He was a high-powered advertising executive who just burned out from too much stress and pressure at work. Even with the extra help, I'm still the one who often needs to make the final decision about something, and yes, that can be a little stressful. See you later."

"Bye, Scott. You take care of yourself!"

CHAPTER ELEVEN

Kelly checked the kitchen as she got ready to lock up for the day and noticed that there was half a cheesecake on the counter. *Roxie must have forgotten to put it in the walk-in. If I take it home I'll probably eat it, and since I'm going to have to fit into a wedding dress in the near future, I probably better avoid it. I know what. I'll take it out to Marcy. I'd like to talk to her anyway and I'm curious if she'll say anything about Gabe.*

It took her about fifteen minutes to get to the driveway that led up to the Black's ranch house. She remembered her conversation with Bonnie the day before and her description of the little rundown shack on the adjoining BLM property. *I thought I knew pretty much everything about the land around here, but I've never seen that old abandoned shack. In fact, I don't think I've ever been on that piece of land. Wonder if I can even get on it. The way she described it, sounds like the shack is about half-way to the point.*

Kelly decided she wanted to try and see if she could find the shack, so she drove past the long driveway that led to the Black's ranch, slowed the minivan down, and looked for a way to get onto the fenced BLM property. A few hundred feet up the highway she saw a small sign with the words "BLM Property – No Trespassing" on it. She drove a few hundred feet past the sign and pulled off onto the shoulder.

"Come on, Rebel. Let's see what this abandoned shack's all about.

Doesn't look like anyone's around, so we shouldn't get arrested. Even though it's gated, I think there's enough of a gap in the gate that we can slip through." They crossed the highway and easily entered the property. Ahead of her she could just make out a small narrow path. "Looks like a footpath. I don't see any tire tracks and anyway, it's too narrow for a truck or an ATV."

Through the heavy forest, she could just make out the cliffs that dropped off dramatically to Jade Cove and the swirling ocean below. Dappled sunlight made it hard for Kelly to see as she made her way along the path. She almost missed the tiny shack just off to the left side of the path. She walked over to it and saw the door hanging at an odd angle from one badly rusted hinge. She gently pushed it open and thought, *Bonnie was right. The only creatures that live here are birds and little critters.* The windows were nonexistent, having been broken out long ago. From the looks of it, no one had been there for a long time. She looked around, curious as to why the old shack had been built in the first place and who had used it. The view of Jade Cove and the ocean beyond it was breathtaking. She stood and looked out through one of the broken windows at the ocean for a long time.

A developer would kill for this land. This view is even better than the one from the Black's ranch house. She walked over to the other window to check out the view from it. At the end of the cove, approximately a hundred yards away, she could clearly see both the shack Jeff had converted into an office and the ranch house beyond it.

Dirt had replaced several of the rotted-out floorboards beneath her. She pulled her attention away from the view, suddenly aware that Rebel was furiously digging in the dirt. "Rebel, stop. What are you doing? Did you find an old bone or some animal?" He looked up at her and barked and began digging again, then pushed something on the ground with his nose. She bent down, picked it up and gasped. It was an expended brass cartridge from a gun.

"Good boy, Rebel. That's really bizarre. From what I remember when my dad used to hunt, it looks like that cartridge came from some type of a hunting rifle. Why would anyone use this shack for hunting? With the steep cliffs, this doesn't seem like a place where game would be found. It doesn't make any sense at all. Why would a hunter be in here?"

She searched the little shack for a few more minutes, but she didn't find anything else. *Well, someone was here and shooting at something, but I don't understand why.* She looked out at the ocean and took another look at the Black's ranch house to see if Marcy's car was there, but no vehicles were parked in the circular driveway in front of the house.

Interesting. Because of the wide panoramic view, whoever was here could have seen what was going on at the Black's house and at Jeff's office, all at the same time. Oh no, she thought. *Maybe it wasn't a deer or some other big game that the hunter was after, maybe it was Jeff. There's no other explanation for the brass casing. Whoever was here might have seen Jeff going to his office and shot and killed him. Maybe that's why the casing is here. Someone shot Jeff right here from this window and didn't want to stay and try to find the casing because they were afraid of being caught. I've got to tell Mike.*

"Rebel, come." They quickly walked back down the path to the road and as she started to get into her van, she saw a note underneath the windshield wiper with writing on it. She slid it out and read the words, "This is a warning. This BLM property is private. Didn't you see the No Trespassing sign? Don't come back." As she held the note in her hand, she realized her hand was shaking.

"Someone saw us go in there, Rebel, and they still may be around. We've got to get out of here. Oh, darn, I forgot I put the cheesecake in the trunk. Well, maybe Marcy's home by now."

She made a U-turn and drove back to the entrance to the ranch driveway. When she got to the ranch house she saw a car she didn't recognize parked in the driveway. *That's funny. I would swear it wasn't there when I looked at the ranch house from the shack. It must have just gotten here.* She got out of her van and as she passed the car, she noticed a bumper sticker on the rear bumper that read "Oregon Needs Lumber." She knocked on the door of the ranch house, but there was no answer. She knocked again, but no one came to the door. She waited for a few minutes and then put the cheesecake back in the trunk and got in the van.

Sure enough if I left it here some animal would eat it. Anyway, it's one of Mike's favorites. She drove back to the highway and was home in a few minutes.

CHAPTER TWELVE

"Mike," Kelly yelled when she entered the house. "You won't believe what I found. Where are you?"

"I'm right here in my favorite spot in the house, looking at the ocean. The sun will set in a few minutes and this time of year I think the sunsets are even more spectacular than usual. Come join me. You sound pretty excited. What's up?"

She walked over, kissed him, and reached into her pocket. "Mike, I found this at the old shack out on the BLM property." She handed him the spent cartridge. "Well, Rebel actually found it and I just picked it up. Look at the bottom of the cartridge. The stamp on it says 30-30. Didn't you tell me that's the caliber of gun that killed Jeff? Do you think this could be from the gun that killed him?"

He looked at the expended cartridge and carefully examined it. "Kelly," he said, looking up at her, "Where, specifically, did you find it?"

Kelly sat in the chair across from him and told him exactly where she was when she and Rebel had found it.

"Okay, let's talk about this," Mike said. "First of all I think there's a very good chance this is an empty cartridge from the gun that killed Jeff. The coroner told me he was shot from a distance because there was no gunpowder residue on him. It's also very possible that someone was waiting in that old shack to shoot Jeff. How far do you think it is from the shack Jeff used as an office to the abandoned shack on the BLM property? Did you say you could clearly see Jeff's office and the Black's ranch house from the old abandoned shack?"

"Yes," she answered. "I could see both of them very clearly. I'd say the old abandoned shack is about a hundred yards from the shack Jeff used for his office, but gauging distances has never been my thing. It could be more or less."

"Let's assume your estimate is close. The killer could have been lying in wait at the old shack because he or she knew that Jeff often left the ranch house at night to go to his office and work. When the person saw Jeff, he or she shot and killed him. Then again, it could have been a random thing, but I find it hard to believe in coincidences like that.

"Mike, there was something else. When I got back to the van after visiting the shack, this note was on my windshield." She handed it to Mike.

"Kelly, when someone left this on your windshield, they were definitely trying to scare you. They either saw you go in there or they saw your car and realized you were in there. It certainly doesn't seem to be a note from the BLM. They would have put it on something more official looking with the BLM logo on it, plus they probably would have gone in there to find you. This concerns me. Did you see any other cars when you went in there?"

"No. I looked carefully before I went in and I'd decided if there was someone else around, I wouldn't go in. I knew I was trespassing. There's a big sign and you can't miss it. I sure didn't want to get arrested for trespassing."

"Well, looks like someone put this on your windshield while you were at the abandoned shack. I wonder if the person who dropped this cartridge in the old shack is the same person who wrote you the note. Maybe someone was afraid you'd find the cartridge. Did you notice anything else?"

"Well, there was something else that was kind of strange. When I got back in the van I realized I hadn't given Marcy the cheesecake that I'd brought for her, so I turned around and went to the ranch house. When I'd looked at the ranch house a few minutes earlier when I was in the shack, her car wasn't there, but I thought maybe in the interim she'd returned. I pulled in and still didn't see her car, but there was another car in the driveway. It had a bumper sticker that read "Oregon Needs Lumber." When I drove in and saw it I thought maybe her car was in the shop for repairs or something, but then I thought a sticker wouldn't be on a loaner car. Anyway, I took the cheesecake from the trunk and knocked on the front door. No one answered, so I knocked again. Still no answer. I turned around, put the cheesecake back in the trunk, and drove here, which reminds me, I need to get it out of the trunk."

"Tell me more about the car that was in her driveway." Mike said.

"Well, it was silver colored and I think it was a fairly late model, but I didn't look at it all that closely other than at the bumper sticker. Why?"

"Depending on what direction the car was coming from, there's a fifty-fifty chance that the same car passed your minivan on its way to the ranch. This time of day there aren't a lot of cars on the highway. I'm just wondering if there's some connection between the car you saw at the ranch house and the note you found, but we'll probably never know."

"Mike, the only person we know who has been out to that old abandoned shack is Bonnie. Do you think she killed Jeff?"

He rubbed his eyes. "I honestly don't know what to think. She knew where the shack was located and she probably had access to one of her husband's hunting rifles. She also hated Jeff because of the damage he was about to inflict on the spotted owls' habitat by building the hotel and spa. She certainly had a motive for killing Jeff. From the empty cartridge case you discovered, I think Jeff was killed by someone who was in the old shack and fired the rifle that killed him. As to the motive and who did it – I don't know. It could be a hunter who mistook Jeff for a deer, although that's a far stretch and it was after the hunting season for deer. What I do know is that you better bring in that cheesecake from the trunk of your minivan. I'd hate to see it go to waste and I'm rather glad Marcy wasn't home, that way I can have it."

"I get the hint. Time to fix dinner. I am so looking forward to this weekend. Sit where you are and I'll call you when it's ready."

"Wait a minute. One more thing. Remember awhile back I bought a gun for you and got you a permit for carrying a concealed weapon. I even took you to the range a few times so you'd feel comfortable with it. I haven't seen it lately, but I'd like you to start carrying the gun with you. Would you do that for me? It sure would make me feel better."

"Sure thing, Sheriff Mike, but I know I'll never need it. Don't forget, I've got Rebel with me."

"I'm well aware of that, but there may be a time when he can't help you. Just say yes and don't fib when you say it."

She made a face at him. "Okay. I will." She realized he was probably right and this time, she didn't even mentally cross her fingers when she made the promise.

CHAPTER THIRTEEN

"Mike, I know planning a wedding is not high on your priority list, but please indulge me. Everyone is wondering why we haven't done anything about setting a date. Can you give me a couple of hours so we can talk about it?" Kelly asked when she'd finished the dinner dishes.

He put down the latest Stephen King novel he'd been reading. "You're right. It's not my number one thing to do and I imagine I'm not the only man in the world who tries to stay uninvolved in wedding plans. It's kind of a guy thing you probably wouldn't understand. Okay, I'm all ears. What do you have in mind?"

"Well, I've been doing a lot of thinking about it. I'd like it to be small. I thought I'd ask Julia to stand up with me and Cash to give me away. Do you think that's schmaltzy and over the top to have your son and daughter that involved?"

"No, I think they'd both be honored. What would you think if I asked Doc to stand up with me? I've gotten to know him over the last few months and we've become friends, plus he adores you. There are several other friends I could ask, but I think it would be a nice touch if I asked him. Would that be okay with you?"

"Oh, Mike, I would love it. He's such a wonderful man and I know he likes you, however, there's one issue I've been hesitant to bring up." She took a deep breath and continued, "I would really like to be married by Father Brown in the Catholic Church. I talked to him today and he said he could conduct the ceremony in the church even though you're not Catholic, since you were baptized as an Episcopalian. When I told him you were divorced, he said he could still conduct the ceremony in the church, but it might really anger some members of the congregation who still feel very strongly that anyone who is divorced should not be married in the church."

"Well, I can understand that. Could he perform the ceremony somewhere else, like here at the house? Maybe we'd just have a small ceremony and then go somewhere for a reception. What would you think about that?"

"Mike, I just want to be your wife. That's far more important to me than where we get married. He did ask me a question I couldn't answer." She looked at him and began to chew on her lower lip. It was an unconscious gesture on Kelly's part and Mike knew she only did that when she was really nervous about something.

"What are you keeping from me, Kelly? Are you going to tell me you're already married to someone else?" he asked, laughing.

"Of course not. Okay, here goes. Father Brown asked if I knew if your ex-wife was alive. He wondered how long it had been since you'd had any communication with her. He said often a former spouse has died and in that case, the surviving spouse can be married in the church."

Mike sat quietly for a few minutes deep in thought. "Kelly, I haven't seen or heard anything about Denise for at least ten years. I know she married that doctor, Brian Hill, the one she met in Las Vegas. I left town when we got divorced and lost track of her. I'm not sure there's any way I could find out anything about her. I'm afraid I can't help you."

"Why don't we try and look her up on Google. I know it's a longshot, but maybe we can find something out."

"Kelly, I'll try it for you, but if that doesn't work, and believe me, I have strong doubts that it will, I think that's the end of the road, but let's find out one way or the other." He stood up from his chair, walked towards the bedroom Kelly had made into her home office, and sat down at her computer. Kelly followed him and sat down on the couch in the cozy office.

Mike pulled Google up on the computer and typed in the words, "Denise Hill." Kelly watched and then saw Mike's eyes widen as he uttered, "What the…"

"Did you find something, Mike? Is something wrong?" He sat quietly looking at the screen intently and sliding the mouse around. After a few minutes he sat back, never answering her.

Kelly got up and walked over to computer to see what had caused his reaction. There on the monitor she saw the headline "Dr. Brian Hill and Wife Killed in Car Crash." She quickly read the article that said they had been returning from a visit to his parents in Northern Oregon when a big rig swerved across the center divider and hit their car head-on. The article went on to say they were killed instantly as was the driver of the big rig. The article was five years old.

"Mike, I'm sorry. This must be hard for you. I know you two were estranged and you'd been divorced for a number of years, but it must be hard to read about her death."

"Not really. About the only emotion I feel is surprise. I told you about how she found the doctor on the Internet and then went to Las Vegas to meet him and how she'd lied to me, telling me she was going to a 'girl's weekend' in Las Vegas. I remember telling you that she filed for divorce as soon as she returned. She got what she wanted – status. A small town sheriff never could give her the status she wanted. No, it was not a good marriage and it ended even worse. It's just really a strange feeling to think that a person you lived with is dead and you didn't know it."

"If you want to be alone for awhile, I'll understand. I'll be in the other room. Come on Rebel."

Rebel sensed something wasn't right with Mike and as Kelly had predicted, his loyalty was beginning to shift to Mike. He stayed in the room with Mike.

A few minutes later Mike walked out of the room with a big smile on his face. "Well, babe, things have a way of working out. Why don't you call Father Brown and tell him we'd like to be married in the church. Looks like with the death of Denise, it shouldn't be a problem. When do you want the wedding to take place?"

"How about on Valentine's Day? It falls on a Saturday. We could get married in the church and have the reception here. I suppose we could have it at the coffee shop, but I think it would be nice to have it here. Let's make it a Celebration of Marriage. If we got married in the morning, we could have the Celebration here from say, one to four. That way people could come and go and we wouldn't have a traffic jam of people. Parking might be a problem, but in a town this small, most people would probably walk here anyway. How does that sound to you?"

"Whatever you want sweetheart, I'm just here to please you and if that pleases you, it will please me as well. Let me ask you a question. Am I going to have to wear a monkey suit?"

"No. I thought we'd wear jeans."

He raised his eyebrows at her. "Kelly, we both have an image to uphold in this town and I'm not sure that's a good idea."

"Oh, Mike," she said laughing, "you are so easy. I'm just kidding! Actually, I thought I'd wear a cream colored or pale colored dress and you could wear a suit. We'll keep it simple. After all, it's a second wedding for both of us, so I don't think I need to be in some fancy white wedding gown with a long train and you don't need to be in a tuxedo. Anyway, Cedar Bay's more of a casual town."

"I'll call Doc tomorrow and ask him. You'll probably want to call your kids and Father Brown. Now, is there anything else you need from me? I'd kind of like to see what's going to happen in the King book I'm reading. I stopped at a crucial place."

"Go on. I'll call them now. Since I don't have anywhere I have to be for the next two days, I'm going to drive up to Portland tomorrow morning and see if I can find a dress. I don't want to leave it to the last minute and things get pretty crazy around the holidays. I'd feel a lot better if I could get that out of the way."

"Portland, tomorrow, okay," he said opening his book and reaching down to scratch Rebel's ears.

CHAPTER FOURTEEN

Saturday morning Kelly luxuriated in bed, finally getting up at 7:30 a.m., much later than her usual time of 5:30 a.m. *I am so glad the coffee shop is closed on the weekends. I feel absolutely decadent getting up at this time of day,* she thought. She put on a robe and walked out to the kitchen where Mike was sitting at the table, drinking coffee and reading his book.

"Mornin', love," she said. "Tell you what. I'll fix breakfast for us before I leave for Portland. I've got some of that salmon gravlax you like so much that's been curing in the refrigerator for a couple of days. It should be ready. I'll slice it ultra-thin and we can put it on some bagels I got at Marsha's bakery yesterday. Sound okay to you?"

"You know it's one of my favorites. Could I have some cream cheese on mine? How about adding a little chopped red onion and chopped hardboiled egg to it? Do you have any mustard and dill? A few capers would really finish it off."

"You're a lucky man to be living with a woman who owns a coffee shop. You know I don't like to leave things in the coffee shop that we can eat here at home on the weekends, so I've got all of them. Give me a couple of minutes."

"Take your time. Matter of fact, I probably won't be doing anything all day but reading. King's got me hooked for sure this time." Rebel put his paw on Mike and looked up at him. "Actually, I think I'll get dressed and take Rebel for a run later on." He looked down at Rebel who was wagging his tail.

I knew it. It's just a matter of time. First he starts secretly giving Rebel treats, and then he runs with him. Rebel's loyalty is definitely shifting away from me. Anyway, I'm glad Rebel has accepted him. It would make it pretty difficult if that ninety pound dog decided he didn't like Mike. Can't decide whether the new puppy should be a Christmas present from me to me or a wedding present from me to me.

An hour later, she walked over to where Mike was sitting, totally engrossed in his book. "I'm leaving now. It takes about two hours to get to Portland. I've got a few shops I really like there. I'll see what I can find. I'm planning on being back here about five this evening. I really don't like driving on highways in the dark and anyway, shopping for just the right thing is always tiring. Wish me luck. Sure would like to find the perfect dress at the first place I go, but that probably isn't realistic."

When she got in the minivan she turned on the radio, listening to soft jazz as she drove. The drive was beautiful, hilly and green, with many trees, creeks, and rivers dotting the landscape. Two hours later she pulled into a parking garage in downtown Portland. *Okay, I can do this*, she thought as she got out of the minivan. *I'm going to trust in the god of wedding dresses for second marriages. With luck, I can be finished in a couple of hours.*

She started at Nordstrom's, looking through rack after rack. No dress spoke to her and asked her to try it on and take it home. She continued her search at two more department stores. Again, nothing. She stopped at her favorite restaurant for an early lunch and had a craft beer and a Reuben sandwich. Refreshed, she was walking down 4th Street when a sign in a boutique bridal shop caught her eye. "Sample Sale – One Day Only." She opened the door of the small shop and realized today was obviously the day of the sale. The store was packed with women, brides-to-be, mothers-of-the-brides, sisters, friends, and anyone else who wanted to help the bride shop for a dress for her big day.

She caught the eye of a frazzled looking sales clerk. "It looks like you're really busy, but I was wondering if you have anything that would be appropriate for a woman my age getting married for the second time. I'm thinking of a cocktail dress or something like that."

The sales clerk looked closely at Kelly, mentally gauging what size she would wear. "You know I do have something I think would work well with your hair and skin coloring. If you'll give me a minute to finish up with the woman standing at the counter, I'll get it for you. Just have a seat and I'll be back in a few minutes." Kelly sat down and began leafing through a bridal magazine that was one of many on the coffee table.

A few minutes later the sales clerk tapped her on the shoulder. "Come with me. I've put the dress I had in mind in a dressing room for you." Kelly followed her down the hall. When she walked into the dressing room she audibly gasped. The most beautiful dress she had ever seen was hanging in front of her. "I definitely want to try it on," she said to the sales clerk. "Thank you for helping me. I'll be out in a couple of minutes."

Kelly pulled the dress over her head. It seemed like the designer had Kelly in mind when he'd designed it. The high-necked long-sleeved sheath was made of champagne colored satin and lace. It fit perfectly. She examined herself from every angle. *I can't think of one reason not to buy it. It's perfect. The only reason may be the price. I probably better see what it costs before I get too attached to it.*

She walked out of the dressing room and over to the sales clerk. "Could you tell me what the price is for this dress?" Kelly asked. Several women in the shop smiled at her. One of them said, "That dress was made for you. You look beautiful." Kelly thanked her and turned to the sales clerk who glanced at the tag on the side of the dress and then pulled a book out from under the counter. She examined it closely, turned several pages, and then looked up at Kelly.

"I think you'll be very happy with the price. The designer is discontinuing this particular line and this dress is the last one. It's on sale and priced at $475.00. I'm sure you'll agree that's a steal."

"I'll take it. Do you have shoes in a size seven that would go with it? I don't want satin dyed shoes. I'd just like something that would work with it, but I could also wear with other things."

"Let me see what I have in the back room. I'll meet you in a few minutes in the dressing room." A few minutes later there was a knock on the door. "I think these would look good with the dress," the sales clerk said, handing Kelly a shoe box containing a pair of very light tan leather high-heeled sandals. Kelly slipped them on and smiled at her.

"This must be my lucky day. They fit like a glove. I'll take them."

"I think this definitely is your lucky day. Those shoes are part of the sale as well. Is there anything else I can help you with?"

"No. This will do it."

Five minutes later Kelly walked out of the shop feeling a huge sense of relief that she didn't need to worry anymore about an important part of the wedding. She was walking by the Hilton Hotel when she saw a silver-colored car that looked exactly like the car she had seen the day before at Marcy's. She noticed the bumper sticker, "Oregon Needs Lumber," and remembered that there had been a similar bumper sticker on the car that had been parked in Marcy's driveway. *That must be the same car*, she thought. *It's too much of a coincidence not to be the same car.*

She was standing a short distance away from the car when Marcy and Gabe Lewis walked out of the hotel. The doorman opened the car door for Marcy then quickly put two small overnight bags in the trunk while Gabe walked around to the driver's side and got in the car. They pulled out of the hotel driveway and merged into the street traffic.

Kelly walked over to the doorman. "Excuse me. I'm sure I recognize that couple that just left, but I can't think of their names.

Do you know who they are?"

"Oh sure. They're here a lot. I don't know what her name is, but his name is Luke Wilson. He's a real good tipper," the tall pock-marked young man in the ill-fitting grey uniform said.

"Thanks. Now that you said it, I remember that's his name. I don't know why I couldn't remember it. Guess I was having a senior moment," she said, walking away from him and heading toward the garage where she'd parked her minivan.

Wow! Everything I've heard must be true. It was Gabe and Marcy and he's using some phony assumed name while he's staying at the hotel with Marcy. That's got to be who was at her house when I was there yesterday. I guess they were too involved with one another and having a little afternoon delight to answer the door when I knocked. Interesting. Wonder if she knows about his financial problems. Maybe I should go out there again and talk to her. I could just be very up front and say I was in Portland and happened to see them.

*****

Kelly thought of the events of the past few days as she drove back to Cedar Bay. It was as if there was a loop of thoughts in her mind that began with finding Jeff's dead body and ended with seeing Gabe and Marcy outside the hotel. As soon as the loop reached seeing Gabe and Marcy, it started over again.

She looked at the clock just above the car radio. *Hmm, it's only 3:00. I told Mike I'd be home about 5:00. I know I'm tense from everything that's happened and I've been promising myself for months I'd go take a yoga class at the retreat center. I think I'll drive out there and see if they have one I can take. If not, I'll still probably feel better just going out there. It's one of the most peaceful places I've ever been.*

Kelly turned up the lane that led up to the center, noticing how well tended the vineyard that surrounded the buildings was maintained. She saw a number of cars in the parking lot and noticed a lot of people walking into the large white wooden building. Originally the mansion of a lumber baron, she thought once again that Scott had certainly picked the right name for it. Big puffy white clouds seemed drawn to the top of the hill where the mansion was and at times it looked like a white cake with white frosting on top of it. Next to the main entrance was a sign that read, "White Cloud Retreat Center – All Are Welcome."

Scott sure has done this tastefully. He told me once how strongly he felt that although he was a Zen Buddhist, the center should be open to all faiths and beliefs. That sign certainly says it all. It's one of the most inviting buildings I've ever seen.

She remembered that she had a small bag in the trunk of the minivan with a yoga mat and some yoga clothes in it. It had been there, unused, for nearly a year. She took it out and joined the people filtering into the building. Once she was inside, she saw a large sign with the class schedules on it. Fortunately a yoga and stress reduction class was beginning in fifteen minutes. She changed into a pair of yoga pants and a T-shirt in the restroom and walked down the hall towards the room where the yoga class was going to be taught. She walked into the room and put $15 in a donation jar located near the entrance to the room.

Around fifty people filled the large, airy room. Orchids, a small fountain, and lighted candles were tastefully arranged in the front of the room, creating a backdrop for the large man who sat facing the class on a yoga mat. As she was placing her mat on the floor at the back of the room, she heard a booming voice behind her say, "Kelly, you weren't kidding when you said you wanted to come out for a class. It's good to see you here and I know you'll be in good hands with my brother. Luke's leading the class today. Remember, I told you he had come here to live with me," Scott said, kneeling down next to her. He smiled at her and waved to a number of other students in the room. "Enjoy the class. I was just walking to my office when I looked in the room and saw you. Better go. Luke's giving me a nod that he wants to start the class." Scott walked out of the room, softly closing the door behind him.

Even though it had been almost a year since Kelly had taken a yoga class, it felt like it was only yesterday. The familiar music, the incense, and the different poses Luke led the class through completely relaxed her mind and body. The class concluded with Luke guiding the students in a breathing meditation for fifteen minutes, and then he lightly rang a small hand-held bell, indicating the end of class. The students opened their eyes and stood up, preparing to leave.

I feel 100% better. Why do I always forget how good I feel when I leave here? What I probably need to do is put a weekly yoga class in red on my schedule and simply make time for it.

She walked out of the old mansion and paused for a moment, admiring the sweeping ocean view. *The lumber baron who original built this mansion sure made a wise choice when he picked this spot for his home,* she thought. She walked to her car, feeling the peace and tranquility that a visit to the always left her with.

CHAPTER FIFTEEN

When Kelly returned home, she carefully hung her wedding dress in the back of her closet. She knew it was an old wives' tale, but she wasn't going to risk losing Mike because he'd seen her wedding dress before the wedding. She knew she'd be looking in the closet from time to time just to admire it. Having the wedding dress made her pending marriage to Mike seem all so real.

She told Mike about the wedding dress she'd bought, Marcy and Gabe in Portland, and taking a yoga class at the retreat center, then she decided to do nothing for the rest of the evening except catch up on some of the food magazines she subscribed to, but never had time to read. At ten that night, she stood up and said, "Mike, I can't make it any longer. I'm tired and I'm off to bed. You're on your own. Even though it doesn't sound like I did much today, it was a tiring day for me. Night."

"Night, sweetheart. Sleep well. I'll join you as soon as this movie I'm watching is over. I have to find out who did it. Probably the sheriff in me."

*****

She rolled over the next morning and saw Mike looking at her. She put her arms around him and kissed him. "Mike, I'm so glad we found each other. I don't think I've ever been happier. I can't wait until I'm your wife, although to tell you a secret, after nights like last night, I'd probably let you live with me anyway!"

"Kelly," he said, his arms tightening around her. "You are absolutely the best thing that's ever happened to me. You know, we never talked about a honeymoon. Is there some place special you'd like to go?"

"No. I just want to be your wife. We can go somewhere in the spring. I'd rather not get involved in making plans for the wedding and a honeymoon all at the same time, and to be honest, after last night, I'm not sure we even need a honeymoon. Let's face it; I think we're already living and enjoying it!"

"Stay in bed," Mike said. "I know Sunday is your favorite day of the week. Tell you what. I'll bring you the newspaper and some coffee. I'll even give you the crossword puzzle and you can do it while I read the rest of the paper. Deal?"

"Perfect, but I need to spend some time at the coffee shop this afternoon. When I left Friday I noticed we were pretty low on a few things. I need to place an order with Lucy at the market and do some prep for the coming week. What are your plans?"

"I want to spend some time working on the Jeff Black case. There are still so many loose ends. For one thing, there are too many people who have a motive to kill Jeff. I'd like to eliminate some of them. I'm just not sure how to do it. Maybe I'll construct some kind of a pyramid chart. Like putting the ones who have the best reason for killing him at the top and working down from there, but right now I'm going to bring us bagels with all the trimmings. That gravlax is about the best thing I've ever had. I don't remember you ever serving it at the coffee shop. Did I miss it?"

"No. I was afraid the name 'gravlax' would scare people off and they wouldn't order it. It shouldn't because it's nothing more than salmon that's cured in the refrigerator with some herbs, salt and sugar. The problem is that gravlax doesn't really sound like a coffee shop kind of thing. I mean everyone knows what caramel rolls are or sausage and gravy, but gravlax, don't know if it would sell."

"Tell you what. Try it and if it doesn't sell, I'll be happy to eat whatever's left over," he said, grinning at her as he left the room.

Two hours later after gorging themselves on gravlax on toasted bagels and working the crossword puzzle, Kelly said, "Mike, I'm going to 11:00 mass. Stay where you are. I'll be back after that. I haven't been able to reach Julia and Cash about the wedding, so I need to call them and make sure they can attend the wedding in February. Cash will probably have to put in his request for leave as soon as possible. I sure hope he can come home for it. It seems like every week some new form of violence erupts in the Middle East. I wish he was stationed a little closer to home."

"Yeah, I know you're worried about him being stationed in such an unstable part of the world, but he's got a lot going for him. He's street smart and that's often more important than having some degree from an Ivy League school. He's going to get out of there and be fine."

"Hope you're right. See you later."

*****

Kelly called Lucy with her grocery order and picked it up on the way to the coffee shop. *Wish there was a Costco or another discount store in Cedar Bay. I know Lucy has to pay to have everything delivered to her, but it sure would make my profit margin larger if I could buy directly from one of them. I appreciate the discount she gives me, but I guess I just don't have the volume to have it delivered directly to me. Oh well, cost of living in a small town. At least most everything else is cheaper than if I lived in San Francisco or Portland.*

Three hours later she'd prepared everything she could for the coming week, caught up on some bookwork, and got the coffee ready for the following morning. *Wonder if Marcy's back from Portland. Never did get a chance to talk to her the other day. I know, I'll get some of my bacon chocolate chip cookies out of the freezer and take them to her. They defrost in minutes and if she doesn't want them, she can always put them in her freezer.*

CHAPTER SIXTEEN

Kelly stood at the front door of the Black's ranch house and knocked on the door. While she waited for someone to respond, she once again admired the beauty of Jade Cove. When Jeff's parents had originally built the house, they designed it so the front of the house overlooked the cove. A circular driveway surrounded it. The view was simply spectacular. In a few moments Marcy opened the door and said, "Kelly, how nice to see you. I wasn't expecting you. I spent a couple of days in Portland at my sister's home and just got back. I'm forgetting my manners. Please come in. Would you like a cup of coffee?"

Sure you were staying at your sister's, Kelly thought. *Probably better not tell her I saw her with Gabe. I'm sure she'd lie and tell me it was someone who looked like her. Well, I'll see what I can find out.*

"No thanks. Marcy, I want to express my condolences. I came by the other day, but you weren't here. I feel so badly for you and Brandon. I know nothing helps at a sad time like this, but I brought you some cookies."

"Thanks, Kelly. You're right, nothing really helps. I was in Portland when my sister called me about Jeff's death and I drove straight home. Brandon came in from Corvallis and spent the night here at the ranch. He returned to school the next day after we made the funeral arrangements. Since Amber's death was so recent, he didn't feel like he could go through another funeral and I agreed with him. That's why we decided not to have a funeral, but instead, simply had Jeff's remains cremated. I think it's probably better for him to concentrate on football and his studies and I'm hoping that will help take his mind off the tragedy."

"That's a good plan for Brandon, but how are you doing? This had to be a shock. I know Jeff had started divorce proceedings, but even so, his murder had to come as a huge shock to you."

"Him filing for divorce and his murder – yes, they both came as a shock. I never thought Jeff and I would be divorced. I loved him dearly and I was always faithful to him. I understand from several people that Jeff thought I was having an affair with Gabe Lewis. He's the lumber guy who lives up in Sunset Bay. Jeff had always been jealous of him because Gabe and I were once engaged to be married. That was before I met Jeff. Jeff never forgot about it. He became obsessed with the idea I was having an affair with Gabe. Really, it was just a figment of Jeff's imagination."

Sure it was, just like you and Gabe were a figment of my imagination yesterday when the two of you came out of the Hilton with overnight bags, Kelly thought.

"I've seen Gabe a few times over the years. He came to see me the other day when he heard that Jeff had died. He offered to give me some money if I needed any. You know he's very wealthy. I told him I was fine, but I'd keep it in mind and if I did run short I'd let him know. Nice to have friends like that, don't you think?"

"Yes. That was a very nice thing for him to do." *Particularly when according to what I read, the guy is having serious financial problems of his own.*

"From what I recall, he's in the lumber business, isn't he?"

"Well, that's putting it mildly," Marcy said, smiling. "In this area of the state, he is the lumber business. He owns a huge lumber mill and thousands of acres of timber so, yes, I guess you could say he's in the lumber business."

"I've been reading there's been a drop in lumber prices the past few years and the industry is in a mini-recession. I understand buyers are importing lumber from Canada because it's much cheaper to buy lumber there, even though it has to be transported a greater distance. Has his business been affected by those developments?"

"Not from what he's told me. In fact, when Gabe first came to see me after Jeff's death, he wondered what I was going to do about building the hotel and spa. I told him I'd received calls from several people who were going to help Jeff finance the construction, but they've decided to pull out because of Jeff's death. Gabe told me he'd like to finance it. Later, after I learned from reading Jeff's will that Jeff had left everything to Brandon since he was going to divorce me, I told Gabe I didn't have the authority to make a decision about developing the property because it was going to become Brandon's. When Gabe learned I wasn't going to inherit the property, he told me he'd like to talk to Brandon about developing the property and becoming his financial partner. So, based on the things Gabe said to me, I didn't think for a moment that Gabe was having financial difficulties. How could he and at the same time offer to become Brandon's financial partner?"

"Marcy, I'm so sorry. That must have been so hard for you when you learned that Jeff had left everything to Brandon."

"Yes, it was. Brandon had an important football game yesterday and he has a couple of exams early this week. I told Gabe it would have to wait until the end of next week. He has really been helpful to me. He even spent an afternoon in Jeff's office, going over his accounts to see if there was anything I needed to know."

"Did he find anything?"

"No, he said everything looked like it was in order. Oh, speak of the devil, here he comes."

She walked over to the door and opened it for him. "Come in, Gabe. I want you to meet someone. Kelly, this is Gabe Lewis. Gabe, Kelly Conner. Kelly owns the coffee shop on the pier. She came out here to give me her condolences."

"Nice to meet you, Kelly. You look familiar. Have we met before?" Gabe asked.

Well, you almost knocked me down when you were hurrying out of the bank and I saw you with Marcy at the Hilton in Portland yesterday.

"No, I don't believe we have. Marcy, I have to be going. I have a large order from the Cedar Bay Market in my minivan and I need to take it to the coffee shop. Gabe, it was nice meeting you."

She walked out and passed what she assumed was Gabe's car in the driveway. On the rear bumper was a bumper sticker that read "Oregon Needs Lumber." Rebel was waiting in the van, standing in his usual guard position on the front passenger seat. When he saw her coming, he jumped in the back.

I know people would probably think I'm crazy for talking to a dog, but I know he understands everything I'm saying.

"Well, Rebel, that was interesting. It seems that Marcy doesn't know Gabe is having financial problems or if she does, she sure didn't act like it. Wonder if what I read is true. Maybe the article about him was wrong although I've heard talk from some of the lumbermen who come to the coffee shop that the lumber business is really down. Several of them have mentioned they're worried they'll lose their jobs."

Rebel looked at her with his head cocked. She was sure he understood every word she was saying.

"I wonder if Gabe can convince Brandon to go ahead with the hotel and spa project, but if more money's needed, where does Gabe intend to get it? And from what Mike told me, Lem would probably be against it and he's the one advising Brandon. This is getting more and more curious! I'll see what Mike has to say about it."

She dropped the items she'd gotten from the market off at the coffee shop and drove home. "Mike," she called out, "we're home. Did you solve the case?"

"Fraid not, sweetheart. I just got home a few minutes ago. I was so frustrated at how many suspects there are and the lack of clues leading to any of them that I threw up my hands and left. How was your afternoon?"

"Well, the good news is I was able to reach Julia and Cash and they'll both be here for the wedding. I talked to Father Brown and confirmed the date with him. He and I had kind of discussed that date when I talked to him a few days ago. I told him what we'd found out about Denise. He was sorry for you, but glad we could now be married in the church without objections from any of the church members. I called Ginger and asked her if she would take care of the guest book signing when people arrive at the church. She and I have been best friends for as long as I can remember and I didn't want her feelings to be hurt because Julia will be standing up with me."

"Kelly, I think you worried needlessly and underestimated Ginger. I'm sure she's just happy that you're happy, but I think it's nice you're making her part of the wedding. It will give her something positive to look forward to after the death of her daughter, Amber."

"I took some cookies to Marcy. I haven't seen her since Jeff was killed and I wanted to express my condolences."

Mike simply looked at her. She squirmed under his gaze for a moment, then said, "Why are you looking at me like that?"

"You just thought you'd take her cookies and express your condolences? Kelly, be honest. We both know the reason you went out there wasn't to give her some cookies. Well, spill it. What did you find out?"

She told him about her conversations with both Marcy and Gabe. "Mike, two things bother me. Number one, it sounds like Marcy has no idea Gabe's in financial trouble, if he is. I sure would like to find that out. And secondly, I don't think this is a good time for Brandon to be making a major decision like whether or not to build a hotel and spa on the ranch property. It almost sounds like Gabe is trying to strong-arm him. Do you think Gabe is doing this to try and get his hands on that three million dollar life insurance policy? I don't know. Maybe he's trying to convince Marcy that the money should be used to build the project instead of saving it to pay for Brandon's education. I know it sounds crazy, but she sure seems to be under his influence."

"Let me think about it," Mike said. "I wonder when he found out she was the beneficiary on the insurance policy? I suppose I could ask her, but that would alert her to the fact that I'm becoming suspicious of Gabe and I'm not sure I want to do that. I'll eat dinner and sleep on it. Maybe the answer will come to me in the middle of the night."

"Marcy told me she'd told him about the insurance money when he brought up the subject of helping to finance the hotel and spa. Mike, one more thing. When I left I walked by a silver colored car in the driveway. I assume it was Gabe's and it had a bumper sticker on it that read, 'Oregon Needs Lumber.' I remember seeing that same sticker on the silver colored car that was in Marcy's driveway the day I visited the old shack and then in Portland when I saw them at the hotel. Do you think he could be the one who wrote the threatening note that was left on my windshield?"

"Could be, Kelly, could be. Don't know how I can get a sample of his handwriting, but I'll keep it in the back of my mind. Now I'd like to seriously think about dinner."

"Okay, let me see what kind of a rabbit I can pull out of my hat tonight!"

CHAPTER SEVENTEEN

The next morning Kelly quietly got out of bed and went into her office. The more she thought about her conversation with Marcy, the more curious she was to find out if what she had read on the Internet was true – that Gabe Lewis was in serious financial trouble. The only thing she could think to do was visit the kennel his wife owned, since she couldn't think of an excuse she could use for visiting the lumber mill. Maybe someone at the kennel could tell her something.

She turned on her computer and booted it up. She remembered that Gabe's wife raised both yellow and chocolate Labrador Retrievers. The chocolate labs were known for being superb hunting dogs, particularly for pheasants and ducks, and while the yellow labs were also fine hunting dogs, it seemed like more and more people bought them to be family pets rather than for their hunting ability.

Kelly pulled up the Lewis Kennel website on her computer. The picture at the top of the site showed a chocolate lab in a marshy area with a duck in its mouth. Beneath it were the words "World Champion Hunting Dogs." The site showed dogs that were currently available, their lineage, the awards the sires and dams had won as well as the dates that future litters would be available. There was even an application form on the website. It was an expensive and impressive site. Below the accomplishments of the hunting dogs were pictures of yellow labs and their contented family owners. There were a number of favorable testimonials from happy owners. Kelly wrote down the telephone number and the address of the kennel, along with the manager's name.

*****

A few hours later while she was at the coffee shop, Kelly said, "Roxie, I need to make a phone call. It looks like this is a pretty good time to do it. I'll be back in a couple of minutes."

"No problem. Take your time. Enjoy the quiet before the lunchtime crowd hits. I can handle it."

I don't know what I'd do without her. It's been ten years now and she's the best waitress anyone could ask for. The customers love her and she has such an infectious warmth about her, I think half of the customers come here just to see her. I'm so glad she and Joe were able to work out their problems with Joe's son, Wade.

She thought back to when a kilo of marijuana had been found in Wade's school locker and he'd been expelled from school, not only for having the marijuana, but for selling it to other students. It had not been an easy time for Roxie and Joe.

Kelly walked into the storeroom, took her phone out of her purse and called the kennel. "Hello, this is Kelly Conner. I was wondering if it would be possible for me to come to the kennel today. I'm thinking about getting a dog for my fiancè for Christmas and I have a number of questions. I've never owned a hunting dog before." She listened to the voice on the other end for a moment. "I can be there about three this afternoon. Would you give me directions to the kennel? I'll be coming from the south."

She wrote down the directions, said goodbye, and walked out into the coffee shop. Just then the front door opened and Doc walked in. "Doc, what are you doing here? You always come at noon and it's only 11:30."

The grizzled retired doctor bent down and scratched Rebel's ears, then took a seat at a table. "Kelly, I wanted to talk to you before the crowd got here. Got a minute?"

"For you Doc, sure. What's up?"

"Well, first of all I want to tell you how honored I am that Mike wants me to stand up with him when you two get married. That's special to me."

"We're both happy you agreed to do it. You're one of our favorite people, but I have a feeling that's not why you wanted to talk to me."

He rubbed his hands together and looked out the window, clearly agitated. In a few moments he turned back to her and said, "No. Something very strange has happened. You know I don't have a television out at the ranch and I rely on my computer to keep me up on the news and current events. You also know all about my past and how the California State Medical Board revoked my license to practice medicine after I was acquitted in the criminal trial for manslaughter in a case involving the death of a young teenage girl who I had performed an abortion on. You also know that the girl's parents sued me in a civil trial and won a three million dollar judgment. I told you how I didn't want to lose all of the antiques and the other assets I'd inherited from my family, so I came up here to live off of the grid. I wanted to make sure they wouldn't be able to find me and so far they haven't."

"Yes. I remember you telling me about it."

"Well, for some reason last night I was playing around on the computer, kind of bored on a Sunday night, and I pulled up the California State Medical Board site. Evidently they have a new chairman who feels there's a critical shortage of doctors. He went through the files of every doctor whose license had been revoked in the last ten years and reinstated two hundred and thirty-three doctors." Doc became very quiet. "Kelly, I was one of them. According to the web site, my license has been reinstated, and I'm free to practice medicine again."

Instinctively, Kelly jumped out of her seat and hugged him.

"That's the most wonderful news I've heard in a long time. I am so happy for you! Now what happens?"

"I don't know. It never occurred to me that something like this would ever happen. After I read it several times not believing what I was seeing, I pulled up the requirements for physicians to practice medicine in Oregon and guess what? Because I now have a valid license in California, a state which has some of the toughest qualifications in the United States for a physician, I can be licensed to practice medicine in Oregon without any problems. It's pretty much a reciprocity thing. All I have to do is fill out a couple of forms and submit them. I guess I'm in shock. I really don't know what to do."

"Doc, have you ever told Liz about your past?"

He looked away from her and rubbed his forehead. He paused and then said, "No. I told her I was a retired physician. She never asked me for any details."

"You like Liz, don't you?"

"Yes. Actually, I like her a lot. Why?"

"Doc, you need to tell her everything you've told me. If your relationship is going to develop, she needs to know about your past."

"Kelly, I've been afraid that if I told her, she wouldn't want me at the clinic any more, and she probably wouldn't want to see me outside of the clinic on a personal basis."

"From what I know of Liz, I really think you're underestimating her. She's not a shallow person. Do you think she's developing some favorable feelings for you?"

"I think so, although our relationship has never gone beyond kissing and hugging. Doesn't mean I wouldn't like it to become more than that. I feel I don't have much to offer a woman. I mean how many women want to be with a grizzled old man who failed as a doctor and a father?"

"First of all you didn't fail as a doctor. I'm sure you were a very good doctor and you told me that what happened to the young woman wasn't your fault and wasn't a result of the abortion you performed on her. Secondly, you didn't fail as a father when your wife divorced you. Your children went with their mother after the trial, but since you've been living off the grid, you haven't pursued finding them and developing a relationship with them. Maybe it's time to do that."

"Kelly, want to hear a crazy pipe dream of mine?" Doc said with a faraway look in his eyes.

"Shoot."

"Well, last night after I found out about it, I thought, wouldn't it be something if Liz and I could operate a clinic together? I could be the general practitioner doctor and she could be the psychologist. Then…" he said, as his voice drifted off.

"What's the then… Doc?" Kelly asked.

"Well, maybe we could kind of make the partnership one that wasn't just work related. Anyway, that's part of the pipe dream."

The door opened and Kelly looked up and saw Liz coming into the coffee shop. "Doc, think your pipe dream just walked through the door." She waved Liz over to where they were sitting.

"Liz, Doc has been telling me some wonderful news. He told me you were the next person he wanted to share it with." Doc stared at Kelly with a thunderstruck expression on his face.

"Doc, I was with a client when you left and I didn't get a chance to thank you for meeting with that very difficult woman I asked you to see. Thanks. And what is this wonderful news?" Liz said, sitting across the table from him.

"Uh, Uh," Doc stammered.

"I've got to go. Roxie's waving at me. See you later," Kelly said, winking at Doc as she got up.

"Roxie, don't take Liz and Doc's order for a little while. I'll tell you about it later."

"No problem. It's your coffee shop. I just follow your orders," she said, grinning.

After Doc and Liz had been sitting at the table for an hour and a half, Kelly told Roxie it was probably time to go over and take their order. She walked back to Kelley and said, "Doc wants to talk to you before he leaves."

"Did he say what it was about?"

"No, he just said and I quote, 'tell her she'll be real proud of me.' He was grinning when he said it and so was Liz."

Doc and Liz stood up and walked over to the cash register as the last diner left the coffee shop. "You two better get out of here. Don't you have patients to see?" Kelly asked.

"Kelly, Liz and I've been talking all this time. I told her everything and she said she already knew all about it. She told me she'd Googled me before she took me on as a volunteer. Can you believe she knew all about me and never said a word?"

Liz smiled up at him and said, "Did you really think I would take someone on to be a volunteer and counsel patients at the clinic I've worked so hard to build up without checking them out? I've known about you right after the first time we talked." She turned and looked at Kelly. "I understand I have you to thank for this and I do. Doc and I've decided he should work at the clinic as a general practitioner. Doctor Amherst has been talking about retiring forever, but he always felt he had a duty to the citizens of Cedar Bay and worried about what would happen to them if he quit. The nearest doctor is up in Sunset Bay. I think he'll be very happy to have a new doctor here in our town."

"That's absolutely wonderful," Kelly said, hugging Doc and then hugging Liz.

"Uh, Kelly, there's a little more to it," Doc said grinning. "Liz, mind if I tell her?"

"No," she said slipping her arm through his. "Actually I know Kelly and I know how intuitive she is. I don't think you need to tell her anything about us. I think she already has the big picture. Thanks, Kelly. I was being way too subtle with Doc. Anyway, I just decided he should be taken off the eligible bachelor list."

Kelly stood looking from one of them to the other. She wiped a tear out of her eye. "This little town has had its share of bad things happen lately, but hearing this wonderful news from the two of you goes a long way to make up for them. I wish you both every happiness in the world. I can't wait to tell Mike. He'll be thrilled!"

Liz walked out the door. Doc followed her, and then turned back, "Kelly, I can never thank you enough. You've changed my life."

"Thanks, Doc, but not so. You've paid your dues and you deserve every bit of this happiness. Enjoy it!"

When she closed the door after them, Roxie was standing there, a smile on her face. "I'm gathering that this is happy news. Would I be right?"

"Roxie, this isn't just happy news. This is simply the best news I've heard in a long time. Sit down for a moment. I'm sure Doc won't mind if I share it with you."

CHAPTER EIGHTEEN

Later that afternoon, Kelly left the coffee shop and headed towards the Lewis kennel location, about forty miles north of Cedar Bay. *I can't believe what just happened with Doc and Liz. I wish I was a writer. That would make a great story with a fairy tale ending. I wonder if Mike will be standing up with Doc at his wedding if this budding romance continues. I'm so happy for both of them. When I left home this morning I thought I'd check out the kennel and see if I could find out anything about Gabe's finances. Maybe I should buy a puppy for Doc as a congratulatory gift. He mentioned one time he was thinking of getting a dog. Don't see him as a hunter even though he's a crack shot. Think a yellow lab family style dog would be more to his liking.*

She followed the kennel manager's directions and forty-five minutes later she saw the sign for Lewis Kennels with a picture of a yellow lab and a chocolate lab on it. She drove down the tree-lined driveway and noticed the large kennels at the end with fully enclosed dog runs leading out from the buildings. It was a much larger operation than she'd expected. She saw an office sign, parked her minivan, and walked into the office.

An attractive middle-aged woman wearing bifocals with a chain attached to them was sitting at a desk looking at a computer, her brow furrowed in concentration. A wall with pictures of hunting dogs on it was behind her desk which was cluttered with framed photos of hunting dogs. Blue ribbons and photos of medals were attached to almost all of the photos.

"Hi, I'm Kelly Conner. I called earlier today and made an appointment to come by and look at some of your dogs. Are you the person I talked to?"

"Yes, I'm the one you spoke with. My name's Angie Scott. I'm the manager and welcome to Lewis Kennels." She pushed her chair away from the computer. "Let me show you around. Are you interested in a chocolate lab or a yellow lab?"

"Well, when I called you this morning, I was thinking of buying a chocolate lab for my fiancé. He's a hunter, but then a friend of mine just shared some great news with me, so now I'm thinking of getting him a yellow lab as a present."

"I'll show you the dogs that are currently available. We have a couple of new litters, but we don't allow our dogs to leave the kennel until they're at least eight weeks old."

"That surprises me. I thought when puppies were six weeks old they were old enough to be separated from their mothers," Kelly said as they walked over to the kennel located to the left of the office.

"Most people do think that and believe me, I get asked that question a lot," Angie said as she opened the door of a kennel building. "We've found puppies do much better when they're separated at eight weeks. It seems those extra two weeks makes a lot of difference in their overall health. Anyway, here's the kennel where we keep the chocolate labs."

They walked down a center aisle with wire enclosures off to each side. In some of the enclosures, dams were nursing pups, in others there were two or three dogs of various sizes and ages.

"You can see we have a doggie door at the back of each enclosure. It opens onto an outside fenced dog run so the dogs are free to go in and out whenever they want. The building is heated as the nights get pretty cool this time of year. We have extra heat lamps that we use for the new litters." She stopped and waved her arm in the direction of the enclosures on her left. "The puppies in these three enclosures are from the same litter. Both the dam and the sire were Bird Dog World Champions. A couple of them are already sold. Mrs. Lewis is checking the references on a couple of other potential buyers. She's very picky about who gets her dogs."

"I'm surprised. I've never heard of a background check being made on prospective purchasers. I thought if someone wanted one of the dogs, they just paid the money, and that was it. Is that practice common for all kennels that breed hunting dogs or is it just the policy at this kennel?"

"Mrs. Lewis owns and runs this kennel. Between you and me, with the lumber industry being in a slump and Mr. Lewis' business in real financial trouble, I would think she'd just want to take the money from any potential buyer, but not her. This kennel is her passion and she feels strongly about it. You can't just buy a dog and take it with you. She requires references and checks them out herself. I've told her we should just sell the dogs and get the money for them, but she won't do it."

"Is she thinking about getting rid of the business?"

"No. Believe it or not, right now it's a lot more profitable than Mr. Lewis' lumber business. I heard he needs a couple of million dollars real soon or he's going to have to declare bankruptcy. The rumor is he could barely make payroll last week. I shouldn't be telling you all of this, but I'm so worried the kennel is going to close if his business goes under. Mrs. Lewis is the most wonderful person in the world to work for. I would hate for her to lose her house or the kennel business because Mr. Lewis made some bad investments."

"I'm getting the feeling you're devoted to her, but not so much him."

"Let's just say from everything I've heard, she deserves a lot better, but then again, you never heard anything from me."

"Don't worry, Angie. I don't know either one of them, so it really doesn't make any difference to me."

Guess the information I discovered on the web was right. According to Angie, Gabe Lewis is definitely having financial troubles.

Sounds of dogs barking and yapping made talking difficult and they walked back to the kennel entrance. "Angie, I don't know anything about hunting dogs, but these dogs are beautiful. How do they get trained to hunt? Do you do something special to get them used to the sounds of gunshots?"

"Buyers have two options. They can train the dogs themselves or we can do it for them. Most of the buyers who train the dogs themselves have had hunting dogs before so they know what's involved. We keep the dogs for six months when we do the training. Mrs. Lewis has two men who do nothing but take the dogs out each day and work with them. The dogs are trained with live birds that are planted in a field so they hear gunshots every day, and eventually they get used to it. When they're returned to their owners, they're fully trained to hunt."

She opened the door to the second building. "This is where we keep the yellow labs. Most hunters prefer the chocolate labs to the yellow labs. The yellow labs are more social and are particularly good with children. We generally sell them to families."

The layout of this kennel was exactly like the one they had just left, but these dogs were far more interested in Angie and Kelly than the ones in the first kennel. Tails wagged and noses were pushed up against the enclosures, begging for human attention.

"These are simply adorable dogs. I can't imagine a child walking out of here without wanting one. It must really be hard for them to wait until Mrs. Lewis checks the parents' references."

"Oh, I'm sorry. I misspoke. She only does that with the chocolate labs. I think every child who comes here would leave in tears if they had to wait to be approved. No, she doesn't ask for referrals for the yellows, but she still wants to meet with the families. I remember once she turned down a family and I didn't blame her. She saw the little boy trying to pull a puppy's tail when she was talking to the parents and they weren't looking. That family left without a dog. Mr. and Mrs. Lewis don't have any children and I kind of think she regards the dogs as a substitute for the children she never had. She's fiercely protective of them."

"Is there a price difference between the chocolate labs and the yellow labs?"

"Yes. The chocolates are much more expensive, even though the yellows are all from champions, just like the chocolates. I think she keeps the prices lower so families can afford them. If a hunter wants a dog from a top hunting lineage, money's probably not a problem for him. I know she really enjoys seeing the happiness that her dogs bring to the families that buy a yellow lab."

"Angie, why is that little puppy at the end all by himself?"

"The people who are willing to spend the money on these dogs, and even the yellows aren't cheap, want to breed them. There's a lot of money in stud fees and litters. As I said earlier, these dogs are all from champions and highly desirable. That poor little guy had one testicle that didn't drop. He can't be shown and should never be bred. That way his unfortunate characteristic will never be passed on to future generations. Mrs. Lewis took him to the vet we use and he said there was an operation a veterinarian could do that would allow the testicle to drop, but he felt it was unethical and he wouldn't do it. She agreed with him. We just found this out yesterday and she hasn't quite decided what to do with him."

"How much do you want for him?" Kelly asked, putting her hand through the enclosure and petting the young pup while he wagged his tail and licked her hand.

"Why, are you thinking of buying him?"

"I wasn't when I walked in, but yes, I think he'd be perfect for my friend."

"Let me call Mrs. Lewis. I'm sure his price would be considerably less than the other dogs because of his condition. Let's go back to the office."

"You go ahead. I'll stay with this little guy and get to know him."

"All right. I'll be back in a few minutes."

Ten minutes later, Angie returned, smiling. "Mrs. Lewis said you can have the puppy for $300.00. You're really lucky. That's much less than what she usually charges, but she doesn't think it would be good for business if people saw a dog with that condition here in our kennel. They may worry that litters from some of the other dogs will have the same problem. She'd like to meet you, but she was just leaving for a meeting with her lawyer. She said you can take the puppy now, if you'd like."

Kelly turned to the puppy. "Well, little guy, guess you were meant to be Doc's." She stood up and said, "Angie, do you have an old dog bed and some dog food I could buy? When I came here I never thought I'd walk out with a puppy and I can't take him to my friend without some food and a dog bed."

"Kelly, you're not the first one to have this problem. I keep a few dog beds here for people like you. I can give you some puppy food as well. Actually, it would probably be better if he stays on the puppy food for a few days before he's introduced to something new. It could be hard on his little tummy and I rather doubt your friend would want to deal with that problem."

"Thank you so much. I can pay with a credit card or check. Which do you prefer?"

"A check would be fine. Just make it out to Lewis Kennels. That way it will at least go in her account, not his."

Ten minutes later Kelly put the dog bed on the back seat of her minivan and went back inside the kennel. She came out holding a squirming little yellow lab puppy that was showering her cheek with wet doggy kisses.

"Well, little guy, hope Doc likes you as much as I do, but if he doesn't, I think you can come home with me. Maybe it's a good thing I stopped on the way here and left Rebel at home. At the very least, I better wash my hands before I see him. He may begin to doubt my loyalty to him when he smells you all over me."

She drove to Doc's ranch and was glad to see his truck parked in front of his house. When he heard the minivan pull into his driveway, he opened the front door, and walked over to it.

"Is there some sort of occasion for this visit Kelly, although you know you're always welcome out here? Seems to me you haven't come out here too often, and when you do, it's usually for something important."

She opened her door and stepped out of the van with a strange look on her face.

"Kelly, are you all right? I've never seen you at a loss for words. Is something wrong?"

She took a deep breath and opened the back door of the van. "No, Doc, everything's fine. I brought you a congratulatory gift and I'm just a little nervous about it." She scooped the wriggling puppy up in her arms and turned around. For a moment there was no expression on Doc's face, and then he broke out in a wide grin.

"He's absolutely beautiful. Kelly, you must have spent a fortune on him." He reached out and took the puppy from her. "Welcome to your new home, boy. Oops, I didn't even check. Is it a guy?"

"Well, kind of. Here's the thing." Kelly explained the circumstances of how and where she'd gotten him at a reduced price. She didn't tell him who Mrs. Lewis was. There wasn't any reason to.

"Fine by me. I've been thinking for a long time that I needed to have a dog. It can get pretty lonesome out here. I just never got around to buying one and it looks like you saved me the trouble. Okay, little guy, I'm going to put you down so you can get familiar with everything and you probably need to take care of some business after that drive from the kennel."

"Doc, I've got a dog bed and some food for him. There's enough puppy chow here for another week or so. The kennel manager said to give him some of this chow for a few days along with whatever you're going to feed him so his stomach doesn't get upset. Where do you want me to put his bed?"

"At the foot of my bed. He might as well get used to me and the ranch from the beginning. I never did like to see a dog sleep in a garage, plus it gets cold out there this late in the year."

Kelly took the bed into the house and walked down the hall to Doc's bedroom. When she returned, Doc was holding the puppy, his face covered with doggy kisses.

"Doc, you've had him for all of five minutes and I think he's already spoiled. Am I right?'

"Yep. It's been a long time since I've had something to care for, now with Liz and this little guy, my world is suddenly changing."

"Any idea what you'll call him?"

"As soon as I saw him, I had one thought. I've been lucky that good things have happened to me in the last few days. I know it's kind of an overused name, but from now on I'm calling him Lucky." He put Lucky down on the floor where he proceeded to sniff his way around the house, going from one room to the next.

"Doc, you may want to close the doors to the other rooms. Fewer things for Lucky to get into."

"Nope. His training has already started."

"The one thing that kind of worried me was what you'd do with him when you go to the clinic and come to the coffee shop for lunch. That's a long time to leave a puppy alone."

"What makes you think I'd leave him alone? You take Rebel almost everywhere you go. From now on I'm taking Lucky everywhere I go."

"Doc, think about it. You're counseling people and pretty soon you're going to be treating medical patients. Do you really think it's a good idea to have a puppy or a young dog in the room?"

"I'll keep a small wire kennel in the room and I'll train him to go in and out of it. If someone's allergic to dogs, I'll have to see them in another room and I'm sure Rebel would love to play with him at the coffee shop."

"Swell. I'm not so sure the customers are going to like two big dogs playing while they're trying to eat. You do realize he'll probably be about Rebel's size when he's fully grown."

"That's no problem. Kelly, Lucky will be so well trained in a few weeks, having him at the coffee shop won't be an issue. And until he is, I'll hold him or put him on a leash. Lucky and I are going to do just fine together."

"Actually, Doc, I think Lucky is the lucky one. Having you for his master is probably as good as it gets for a dog."

"Thank you, ma'am. Now get out of here. Time to start training Lucky. Does Mike know about this?"

"No. I didn't even know this was going to happen until I saw Lucky. I better leave. It's been a busy day and I've got a lot to tell him." She walked over and instead of kissing Doc on his cheek, she kissed Lucky on the top of his head. "Goodbye little guy. Welcome to your new home."

I'm kind of sorry I didn't keep him. Rebel's getting more and more attached to Mike. Maybe I should get a puppy and if I decide to get one, I think I know where to go and what breed to get.

*****

"Mike, I'm home. You won't believe what happened today."

"I'm glad you're home, I was getting worried about you. I tried to call you on your cell phone, but it was turned off. Where have you been?"

"Well, I was so happy for Doc I bought Lucky for him and…"

"Stop." He held up his hand. "I don't have a clue who Lucky is and why you bought Lucky for Doc and why you were happy for Doc. Kelly, start at the beginning."

She told him everything, starting with when Doc had come to the coffee shop that morning and finished with driving home from Doc's a few minutes ago.

"Kelly, that's wonderful. I'm really happy for him. I've met Liz a few times. Actually, she's helped me with a couple of people I made a judgment call on. Told them they had a choice. They could see a psychologist or be tried for a crime. While she can't tell me the details of her sessions with them, she does tell me whether or not they're continuing to see her and how they're doing. And to think that Doc will be practicing medicine again! I'm sure Dr. Amherst will be happy to hear that. He told me once how much he wanted to retire, but as the only doctor in Cedar Bay, he didn't want to abandon his patients. Now he can simply shift them over to Doc. Everybody wins. I'd say you had a good day. Now, let's talk about dinner."

"Sheriff, if it wasn't for the ring on my finger I'd swear you care more about food than me, but then again, I've always heard that the way to a man's heart is through his stomach. Sure think it might apply to you. I'd like to ask you if you'd still want to marry me if I wasn't such a good cook, but I don't think I want to know the answer to that one. I remember something Lem said once about a lawyer never asking his client a question unless the lawyer knew the answer, because many a case is lost when the client blurts out something other than what the lawyer is expecting. I think it might be applicable here."

"Why, Kelly," Mike said with a playful shocked expression on his face. "I can't believe you'd even think such a thing."

"Let's put it this way, Sheriff Mike, I'm not asking the question. As for dinner, how does stuffed pork chops, creamed spinach, a fresh garden salad, and that killer chocolate cake I make sound to you?"

"Kelly, would you think I'd become senile if I started drooling?"

"No. I'd say you were just a man who appreciates good food."

CHAPTER NINETEEN

A few minutes before noon the following day, the door to Kelly's Koffee Shop opened and in walked Doc with Lucky on a little blue leash. It was obvious to Kelly that he'd been one of the first customers at the pet store that morning. Everyone in the coffee shop oohed and aahed over Lucky and told Doc how cute he was. Rebel got up from his customary place on his bed near the cash register and sniffed the little puppy. Satisfied he wasn't a threat to Kelly he got back on his bed and watched the puppy with a look of disdain in his eyes.

"Kelly, how about putting a little water in a saucer for Lucky? He's had a busy morning at the clinic. Poor dog has had people fussing over him all day. I think he's ready to spend some serious quiet time back at the ranch."

"Here you go Lucky." Kelly put the dish on the floor in front of him. "Doc, it may have been awhile since you've had a dog, but you need to make sure he's got water. Poor little guy seems to be really thirsty."

"I know, Kelly, but remember, the more he drinks, the more I have to get up and let him out and he's too little to go outside by himself. Plus, we've got coyotes around the ranch and he'd make a nice appetizer for one of them."

"Well, Doc, you better get used to it. That's part of owning a dog. How did he do last night?"

"Actually, better than I thought he would. I only had to get up once in the middle of the night to let him out and then again at dawn. I don't think housebreaking him will be a big problem. I'm going to have to fix a couple of holes in the fence to keep the coyotes out. Other than that, I think we'll get along just fine. Was Mike surprised you got me the puppy?"

"Not only surprised, but grateful I didn't come home with one. He thinks Rebel is great, but he has mixed feelings about puppies. Thinks they're cute, but knows they require a lot of work. He's not sure he's up to it. He likes to have a dog that's already trained. He doesn't know it yet, but I'm getting a puppy when we get married."

"As well trained as Rebel is, someone must have spent a lot of time working with him. I remember you telling me you got him when a drug agent was killed and Rebel had been trained by the agent as his drug-sniffing dog," he said, reaching down and petting Lucky whose head was on his shoe. In a minute the little dog was snoring softly.

"If you've got a minute, Kelly, I'd like to talk to you."

"Again?" she asked, sitting across from him. "After everything that happened yesterday, I didn't think you'd need to talk to me for quite awhile."

"This is about Brandon Black. He called me from school this morning and asked if I had a minute to talk to him. His dad had told him about his meeting with me and how much he trusted my judgment. Brandon said if his dad trusted me that much, he'd feel comfortable talking to me about something that was worrying him. He was at the ranch Sunday morning and Marcy was pretty excited because she'd received the proceeds from the insurance policy. Evidently she didn't think she'd get it that fast. He said what worried him was that Gabe had come to the ranch that morning. He doesn't like Gabe at all, because Jeff was honest with him and told him that the reason he was divorcing Marcy was because of the affair she was having with Gabe."

"I wondered if Brandon had heard about it. I'm not surprised that Jeff told him, considering how close they were."

"Anyway, Brandon was studying for a test he was going to take yesterday. He told me he got hungry and on his way to the kitchen, he overheard Gabe ask Marcy what she was going to do with the insurance money. She told him she was going to cash the check at the bank the next day, which would have been yesterday. Gabe told her he'd like to go to the bank with her, that he could probably help her invest it and make a far better return on it than she'd get at the bank. Evidently she didn't want to, but in the end she agreed to do it. Brandon's worried that she might have given Gabe some or all of the money."

Doc doesn't know about Carlos. I wonder if Marcy cashed the check, hoping to pay him off.

"From everything I've heard and read," Kelly said, "Gabe is having some terrible financial problems. If he could convince Marcy to give him the money, that sure would take care of his financial problems. I've heard he needs a couple of million dollars, like right now."

He looked at her quizzically. "How could you possibly know that?" he asked.

"Someone mentioned it to me, but for the life of me I don't remember who it was," she said, mentally crossing her fingers. "What did you tell Brandon?"

"I told him I'd see what I could find out, although I don't know how I'm going to do that. I've met Marcy maybe once and I sure couldn't just go out to the ranch and ask her if she'd given Gabe the proceeds from the insurance policy."

"No, of course not. Let me think about it. Maybe there's some other way we could find out. Doc, I'd love to stay and talk, but the coffee shop is filling up and I stranded Roxie yesterday. I can't do it to her two days in a row. I want to keep her happy and making her work twice as hard is not going to keep her happy. I'll talk to you later. You and your new little friend here have a good rest of the day."

"Kelly, have you been to the bank today?" Roxie asked. "We're getting really low on change in the cash register. For some reason, almost everyone who's come in today has paid with a credit card."

"No, it kind of slipped my mind. I'll do it right now. Even though we have a crowd, it seems under control and I'll just be a few minutes. Thanks for the reminder."

Kelly opened the door of the First Federal Bank and waved to Patti, her friend from high school. "Hi, Patti. What exciting things have happened at the bank this week?" she asked, walking over to her and pulling an empty money pouch out of her large tote bag. "I need to get some cash. Seems like everyone's paying with credit cards and when we do have to make change, it's getting to be a problem."

"The exciting thing was that we're almost out of cash, too. One of our customers cashed a huge check yesterday. The bank manager called our parent company to see if we could cash it immediately or if we should put our usual hold on it, but since our parent company was the maker of the check, we didn't have a choice. Left us really stranded. I mean three million dollars is a lot of money."

"Wow! That is a lot of money, particularly for a bank in a small town." Kelly said, handing her a withdrawal slip for $200.00. "Any chance I can get that much cash out of my account?" she asked with a mischievous smile on her face. *And I know who cashed it. Now I wonder who has the money. Maybe I should go out to Marcy's and see what I can find out.*

"Here you are, Kelly. See you in a couple of days."

*****

Kelly left the coffee shop a few minutes after Roxie, Madison, and Charlie had left for the day. "Come on, Rebel. I need to pay Marcy a visit. I have no idea what I'm going to say, but I have a hunch I need to go out there."

A few minutes later when she turned up the long driveway that led to the ranch house, she saw a large SUV in the driveway with the words "Lewis Kennels" on it. She quickly stopped, put the minivan in reverse, and drove back about two hundred feet. She parked the van in a small clearing off to the side of the driveway. "Rebel, watch the van. I have a feeling this isn't going to take too long."

Kelly opened the van's door and walked next to the gravel driveway in the grass, trying to make as little noise as possible. The back of the house was surrounded by trees which hid her from view. When she got close to the house she heard raised voices coming through an open window. She looked around and didn't see anyone.

That's got to be Mrs. Lewis' SUV. Gabe has a silver colored car and anyway, he wouldn't be driving the Lewis Kennels car here. Angie said it was Mrs. Lewis' business. I'm sure he wouldn't normally even have access to her car.

She crouched down under the window and could clearly hear two raised voices. She listened for several minutes.

"I'm not stupid. Everyone knows you've been having an affair with my husband. I saw a lawyer yesterday and started divorce proceedings against him. I don't want Gabe to get my kennel business. He's in such bad financial trouble he's been begging me to give him the money I've earned from it, but there's no way I'm going to do that. He may have told you he loves you, but he just wants your money. Trust me, you're not the first. Between bad investments he's made and the slump in the lumber industry, he needs money just to meet payroll this week. Bet he didn't tell you that because it's not too romantic."

"Get out of my house, you jealous liar. You're crazy. Gabe's offered to help me if I have any financial needs and he wants to talk to Brandon about becoming his partner and building the hotel and spa my husband was going to build here at Jade Cove before he died."

"If you really believe that, you deserve him, but remember this, he's a lying, cheating, conniving business failure who will suck you dry and leave you penniless and out on the street. Don't bother to show me to the door. I can find my own way out." She slammed the front door shut and ran to her car. Seconds later Kelly heard the sound of the engine roaring as the Lewis Kennels SUV sped down the driveway, scattering gravel behind it. Kelly quickly ran back to where her van was parked in the small clearing, her heart beating wildly.

It looks for sure like Marcy is the one who got the money out of the bank, but it sounds like she may not have given it to Gabe yet. I wonder if she's going to do it after what Mrs. Lewis just told her. And if Gabe needs the money to make payroll this week, something's probably going to happen pretty soon. Mike needs to know about this.

CHAPTER TWENTY

"Hi, Kelly. I just made a pot of coffee. It's getting cold out and it sounded good. Care to join me?" Mike said, as she and Rebel came through the front door.

"Sounds great, although I'm so wound up right now, I'm not sure I need any. I probably should go out to the retreat center and take a yoga class, but it's too close to dinner. I've got so much to tell you, I don't know where to start."

"Start at the beginning," Mike said, handing her a cup of coffee. "That's usually a good place."

Kelly told him about Doc's conversation with Brandon and her visit to the Black's ranch. When she finished, he sat silently, trying to make sense of what she had told him.

"I had an interesting day as well. Brandon hasn't been high on my list of suspects, but I wanted to cross all the t's and dot all the i's, so I called the resident adviser at the dorm where he's living at Oregon State University. He confirmed that he'd seen Brandon the afternoon and evening of Jeff's death. He was studying in his room in the afternoon and was at dinner that evening. Brandon was definitely in Corvallis at the time of Jeff's death. Based on that information, I've eliminated him as a suspect even though he profits from Jeff's death more than anyone else. As close as Brandon and Jeff were, I never did see him killing his dad."

"I'm glad. I never really thought Brandon was the killer, but that still leaves us with several suspects. It's almost as if we need to determine who the killer is by process of elimination."

"Kelly, I think I've mentioned this before. It's not 'we' who need to do this, it's 'I' who needs to do this. Am I making myself perfectly clear?'"

"Of course. I meant you, it's just that we're talking, so the 'we' came out."

"Uh-huh." Mike raised his eyebrow and looked at her. "Let me continue," he said, giving Kelly a dirty look. "I found out that Bonnie was attending a public hearing on endangered species at the capitol in Salem the afternoon and evening of Jeff's death. Actually, she spoke at the hearing. The meeting lasted into the early evening hours. Several people confirmed she was there for all of it, so that eliminates her. Another thing that bothered me about her was that Jeff was killed with a bullet from a hunting rifle. I never could see Bonnie with a hunting rifle. It goes against everything she speaks out about. Someone told me she was a strong advocate for completely outlawing guns. She doesn't think anyone except those connected with law enforcement should own one. She's also against hunting. Sort of a strange position for her to take given the fact her husband is a hunter and gun owner, but then again, Bonnie has always been a bit strange. Anyway, for those reasons, I've pretty much eliminated her as a suspect. I know Brandon or Bonnie could have hired a third party to kill Jeff, but I don't think so. "

"Okay, so we, whoops, sorry Mike, so you still have several suspects. Let's see, there's the Indian angle, Marcy, and Gabe. Is that everyone?"

"You left out Carlos Delgado. We know he's a shady drug cartel type of character, but I can't see how he would profit from Jeff's death. If anything, the money he was getting from Jeff dries up with Jeff's death. I can't think of anyone else. The Indian angle still interests me. I know they can't have firearms on the reservation, but as I mentioned before, you can keep a firearm under a blanket in your car or anywhere else, for that matter. The tribe members are known for being excellent hunters and I imagine a number of them do have access to rifles. If one of the members of the tribe did it, I wouldn't know where to even start trying to figure out which one it was."

"I've gotten to like Chief Many Trees," Kelly said. "I really believe if he thought one of the members of his tribe had done it, he'd tell you. He cares so much about his tribe. Even though he hated Jeff for planning on building the hotel and spa on his property and in his words, 'defiling the tribe's ancient burial grounds,' I think you should eliminate him based on his opposition to anyone having a gun on the reservation," Kelly said.

"Well, if I eliminate him and the members of his tribe, that leaves me with Marcy and Gabe. Marcy had a good reason to kill Jeff. He was divorcing her and she was going to lose her home. I don't think I've ever heard of Marcy working or having an occupation to fall back on. I imagine she was terrified about what the future might hold for her and what her life was about to become. At her age, sponging off her sister in Portland wouldn't seem like a pleasant prospect for a proud and pampered woman like Marcy. Don't forget that I asked her if she had a gun and she said she did."

"Yes, and a three million dollar life insurance policy provides a very good motive. That would go a long way towards keeping the wolf from her door. We know she was having an affair with Gabe, but I keep coming back to her role as a mother. Remember, I mentioned early on that I think she's a very good mother. When Amber was murdered, she was really there for Brandon. I was the one who told him Amber had been killed and she was as supportive as any mother could be. Also, she knew how close Brandon and Jeff were and how it would hurt Brandon if something happened to Jeff. And if she is the killer, she had to be thinking about what would happen to Brandon if she was convicted of being Jeff's murderer. She would go to prison for life and Brandon would essentially become an orphan. I don't think she would do that to Brandon, but I could be wrong," Kelly said.

Mike continued talking. "So that leaves us with Gabe as the prime suspect. We know he's in real trouble with his business. It's totally dependent on the lumber industry being healthy. He's been hit twice with the slowdown in the lumber business. Once from getting less money for the trees he harvests from his acreage, and secondly, from diminishing business at his lumber mill. We also know he's having an affair with Marcy. Maybe he didn't have an ulterior motive for having an affair with Marcy, but given his desperate need for money, I doubt it.

"We know that the two of them were engaged before he married the Sunset Bay woman, so it wouldn't be that strange for them to resume their prior relationship. Happens a lot. The attraction is still there. Look how many high school lovers reconnect at a class reunion. What we don't know is whether he's seriously in love with Marcy. Maybe he was getting ready to divorce his wife and marry Marcy. Maybe he hoped Marcy would get half of the Jade Cove property if she and Jeff got divorced and he could sell it or subdivide it. It certainly is valuable land."

"Well, if that's true, it all fell apart when Marcy was served with the divorce papers. I remember that she said she'd told Gabe everything Lem had told her when he served her with the papers and that would include the information about the life insurance settlement. Then, don't forget, they were at the bank and found out she'd been left out of the will."

"I haven't forgotten that," Mike said, "but remember, they found out about the will after Jeff's death."

"That's true. So if Gabe killed Jeff to marry Marcy and get the property, thinking she would inherit it, that plan fell completely apart when Gabe found out Jeff had left everything to Brandon. The only thing left that would interest someone in dire financial straits would be the proceeds from the life insurance policy," Kelly said.

"Let's face it, Gabe is definitely desperate, and from what you overheard, he's probably going to do everything he can to get the insurance money from Marcy. I also keep thinking back to when she told me about Carlos. I wonder how he figures into this. He said he'd return and when he did, he wanted his money or else. Remember, he was serious enough about it to have one of his men draw blood from Marcy's throat when he held a knife on her. Either way, Marcy could be in danger from Carlos or in danger from Gabe. I wonder if anyone is at the ranch with her."

"I don't think so," Kelly said. "When I went out to the ranch this afternoon, I only heard two voices. Now that I think about it, her sister wasn't there when I took the cookies to Marcy Sunday afternoon. She must have just stayed a day or so. Somewhere I remember hearing that she's much younger than Marcy and has small children. She probably had to go home and take care of them.

"What do you say we call it a night? I need to fix dinner. I brought some chicken pot pies home from the coffee shop. I thought we'd have those and some cornbread I can reheat. It's been a tiring day and I'd prefer to have some leftovers rather than cook a full meal, if you don't mind."

"Kelly, what you call leftovers everyone else would call some of the best food they'd ever eaten. Sounds great!"

"Almost forgot the best part, Mike. I made some caramel sauce today and served it to customers over a vanilla cake with ice cream. We can finish up with that."

"Well, woman, quit talking about it and just do it. This man is starving."

Forty-five minutes later Mike sat back and rubbed his stomach. "Kelly, that was fantastic. I'm stuffed and happy. Think I'll watch a little TV and then head for bed. How about you?"

"I'm whipped. I'll clean up these dishes and join you in a few minutes."

Mike's phone rang as he stood up from the table. "This is Sheriff

Mike." He listened to the voice on the other end of the phone. "What time did he say he'd be there?" He listened again and looked at his watch. "On my way, Marcy. See you in a few minutes. If he gets there before I do, try to stall him."

"What..." Kelly started to ask, but Mike held up his hand and punched in a couple of numbers on his phone.

"Rich, need you out at the Black's ranch ASAP. No siren. A man from Mexico by the name of Carlos Delgado is on his way to Marcy's and he's probably armed and dangerous. There's a turn-out next to the driveway, about two hundred feet back from the ranch house. Park there and walk up to the house. I'll meet you there."

"I'm going with you, Mike," Kelly said.

"No, you're not. I want you to stay here," he said as he slammed the front door shut, jumped in his car, and took off at a high rate of speed.

Oh, yes, I am too going to go. "Come on, Rebel." She grabbed the pistol from the drawer where she kept it and she and Rebel were in her minivan in seconds. *Mike, I know you think you don't need my help, but you're wrong.*

CHAPTER TWENTY-ONE

Kelly was driving so fast she was afraid she'd catch up to Mike and she knew he wouldn't be happy if he saw her, so as soon as she could, she pulled off onto the service road that paralleled the highway north of town. By now it was after 8:30 at night and there was little or no traffic on the seldom used service road.

Ranchers were the only ones who were usually on it and then only until they could get out on the highway. There were periodic entrances to the highway and she remembered there was one that was just a little south of the Black's ranch. She came to the stop sign, looked to her left, and didn't see Mike's car. She doubted if Mike would pay much attention to a car driving on the service road.

Good. Well, I either beat him here or he beat me. Either way, that's fine with me. It's just a few hundred yards to the driveway that leads to Black's ranch.

She decided to drive past the driveway and park the minivan behind a stand of trees so Mike wouldn't be able to see her van. When she got to the stand of trees in front of the BLM land she noticed a silver colored car already parked there. She pulled in next to it and got out. A few moments earlier, she'd turned off the lights on her minivan so she wouldn't attract attention, but in the moonlight she could clearly make out the bumper sticker on the rear bumper of the car that read "Oregon Needs Lumber."

If my eyes aren't deceiving me, that's got to be Gabe's car. It's the exact same bumper sticker I saw on his car when he and Marcy came out of the hotel in Portland and when the car was parked in her driveway. If it's his car, why would he park here and not in Marcy's driveway? That's really odd.

She took the gun out of her purse and put it in her jacket pocket along with the keys to the van. "Rebel, come," she whispered, opening her door and motioning for Rebel to get out of the car on her side. *I know Gabe's desperate and if he's parking here and not in Marcy's driveway that concerns me. I'm glad I thought to bring a gun. I don't trust that man. I wish I knew if Marcy has given him any of the money from the insurance proceeds, but with Carlos coming, I'd think she'd have to keep half of it to pay him off.* Kelly carefully walked up to the silver colored car, gun drawn, and looked inside. There was no one in it.

The stand of trees was next to the gate that led to the Bureau of Land Management property. She'd slipped around that gate several days earlier when she'd found the abandoned shack.

There can only be one reason why Gabe's car would be parked here, Kelly thought. *He must have entered the BLM property and if he knows about the shack, I'd bet anything Gabe is the one who killed Jeff. Gabe's a hunter and Jeff was killed by a bullet from a hunting rifle. It all makes sense now, but why would he come back here tonight? I hope he doesn't plan on doing something to Marcy.*

She motioned for Rebel to follow her as she slipped around the gate and started to walk along the narrow path that led to the abandoned shack. *I'm so glad I changed into tennis shoes when I got home. At least I'm not making any noise while I'm walking.* It was deathly quiet on the path and even the night animals were silent.

This is really odd. Animals seem to have an uncanny sense regarding danger and I'll bet if Gabe's out at the abandoned shack, they sense something is wrong. Maybe that's why I don't hear any sounds. If he's there, and I bet he is, he must have scared them off.

After walking quietly about a hundred yards along the dark narrow path, she came to a spot where she could just make out the old dilapidated shack ahead of her in the moonlight. She was about twenty feet from it when she heard a loud gunshot come from the shack. She jumped behind a tree and pulled on Rebel's collar, motioning for him to stay behind her. She stood and waited for whoever was in the shack to come out, her gun aimed at the shack's door. At the far end of the cove she could clearly see a woman who appeared to be Marcy come out of the ranch house. Seconds later she ran back into the house and Kelly heard the front door slam with a loud bang. Sounds of a man's voice swearing came from the shack. A few moments later she recognized Gabe as he ran out the door holding a rifle.

"Drop it or I'll shoot," Kelly yelled. "Rebel, go!"

Gabe dropped his rifle while Rebel stood next to him, growling and waiting for Kelly to give him the command for attack.

"Gabe, one move and that dog will have you on the ground and I won't be responsible for what he's going to do to you," Kelly said. "I know you killed Jeff with that rifle. You're a hunter. It all makes sense now."

"Not only will Rebel take you to the ground, but I'll shoot to kill. Understand me?" Mike said in a loud commanding voice as he seemingly appeared out of nowhere. He swiftly walked over to where Gabe was standing and said, "Kelly, keep me covered while I handcuff him." When he was finished he got out his phone and made a call. "Rich, what's happening at the ranch house?" He paused. "Carlos has been shot and killed? Is Marcy okay?" He listened to Rich. "Call the coroner and then drive north about two hundred feet. You'll see my car. Got someone who needs to go to jail."

"Mike, what are you doing here? How did you know I'd be here?" Kelly asked, her voice beginning to break from stress and tension.

"I was just getting ready to turn into the Black's driveway when I saw something shining in the moonlight a little farther up the highway. I decided to drive up there and see what it was because I knew Rich would be at the ranch by now and could probably handle Carlos by himself. I saw your car and a car I assumed was Gabe's from its color and the unique bumper sticker on its rear bumper. I didn't think anything good could come from that combination, so here I am. And it looks like I may have gotten here just in the nick in time."

He turned to Gabe. "Want to tell me why you're here, why you have a rifle, and why you killed Carlos? And while you're at it, I'd like to know why you killed Jeff. Be willing to bet my sheriff's badge that there will be a match on the bullet that killed Jeff and your rifle. Now I understand why there was no gunpowder on Jeff. You shot him from the same place where you just shot Carlos, right here from this old shack." He turned and looked at the ranch house and Jeff's office. "Yeah, you've got a clear line of fire from here. It's only about one hundred yards. That would be an easy shot with a high-powered hunting rifle."

"I want my lawyer. I've got nothing to say to you."

"Gabe, I'm going to be honest with you. I'll bet anything that your rifle was responsible for killing Carlos and Jeff. That probably means you'll be headed to prison for life. I may be able to help get your sentence reduced if you tell me why you did it."

"I told you before. I've got nothing to say. I'm entitled to a phone call and you can talk to my lawyer from now on."

"Pal, from what I hear about your lumber business, I don't think you're even going to be able to make bail, much less hire a lawyer to defend you in a capital murder case. I'm giving you one last chance. Why were you here and why did you kill Carlos?"

"Sheriff, maybe you need to see someone about your impaired hearing. Maybe you didn't hear me the first two times I told you that I've got nothing to say to you."

Mike turned to Kelly. "Tell me what you saw and heard."

"I heard a gunshot come from the shack, then Gabe started swearing. I heard him say something like 'Marcy, get back out there. I need that money and the only way I'm going to get it from you is when you're dead,' and a few moments later, he ran out of the shack. Is Marcy okay?"

"Yes, Rich got there just in time. Gabe's aim with his rifle was deadly accurate. Carlos died instantly from a gunshot wound to his head. From what you heard, I can only assume that Gabe was planning on killing Marcy as well, but she ran back in the house before he could get off a shot at her. He probably figured if he killed them both he could quickly drive over to the house and steal the cash Marcy was going to give to Carlos. I need to talk to her to see if Gabe threatened her. Maybe she refused to give him the money."

"Poor Marcy. She must be terrified."

"Gabe, start walking towards the car. Rebel, walk behind him. One false move, Gabe, and I shoot and the dog goes for your throat. Got it? Kelly, give Rebel the right command for that." He took a handkerchief out of his pocket and carefully picked up Gabe's rifle from where it was lying on the ground.

"Rebel, follow, guard!" Kelly said. Rebel walked behind Gabe as the four of them made their way along the narrow path to where the cars were parked. Rich pulled up just as they reached the highway.

"Get in," Mike said opening the back door of the deputy sheriff's car. "Rich, don't think this will be a problem since he's cuffed and you have the steel grate separating the two of you, but I'd feel better if you took Rebel with you. He can sit in the front seat and he's trained to attack if Gabe tries anything when you walk him from the car into the jail. I need to talk to Marcy. I'll meet you at the jail in a little while. Wait until I get there to give him his phone call."

He turned to Kelly. "I know it wouldn't do me any good to tell you to go home, so I'll ask you to follow me to Marcy's. I want to talk to her and see what happened before Rich got there."

"Thanks, Mike, but you have to admit, I did a pretty good job."

"I'll give you that. I'm just glad we've spent a little time at the gun range lately. I know you didn't fire the gun I insisted you have, but I'm glad you had the sense to bring it with you."

"Thanks, Sheriff Mike. I appreciate your faith in me," she said sarcastically. "After all, I was the one who had the gun on Gabe when you walked up."

"Kelly, Kelly, Kelly. You're driving me nuts. I'm not sure you're making my job any easier with me having to constantly worry about your safety."

"Mike, this is the last time I'll do anything like this. I just wanted to help you and so help me, I think I did."

"This is not the time or place to discuss how you're going to act in the future when it comes to my investigations. We'll talk about it another time. Right now you can follow me in your van."

"Yes, sir!"

Well, I don't care what he thinks. It was me holding the gun on Gabe when Mike walked up, not him holding the gun on Gabe when I walked up. I'll probably have to act like I really mean it when I say I won't get involved next time, but I'm two for two now. I found Amber's killer and now I found Jeff's. He can say anything he wants, but those are the facts.

She pulled in Marcy's driveway and parked next to Mike's car. They both walked up to the front door. Mike knocked and said in a loud voice, "Marcy, it's Mike. Everything's okay now. Please open the door. Kelly's with me and we need to talk to you."

The door opened and Marcy stood there, pale and trembling. She was clearly in shock. Tears streamed down her cheeks. Kelly walked past Mike and took Marcy by the arm to support her. She looked like she was about to faint. Kelly led her to the nearest chair. "Marcy, sit down. What's your sister's number? I'll call her and tell her to come immediately."

Marcy shakily gave her the number and Kelly called it. "She'll be here as soon as she can. Her husband had a meeting tonight and she doesn't have anyone to watch the children, but as soon as he returns she'll drive over from Portland."

"Marcy," Mike said, "I need to know everything that's happened out here in the last few hours. I've arrested Gabe Lewis for the murder of Carlos and I'm sure Gabe was the one who murdered Jeff. Tell me everything you can remember."

She started sobbing. "Mike, are you sure it was Gabe? I can't believe he'd do something like that even though he was really mad at me." She wiped the tears from her cheeks with a tissue Kelly had given her.

"Why was he mad at you?" Mike asked.

"Gabe came over earlier this evening and told me he'd had a meeting this afternoon with a man who handled his investments. He told me the man worked for himself and wasn't part of a big company or anything. He said he was an investment genius. Gabe said he'd made far more money investing through him than he would have if he'd gone with some big investment firm. He told me if I'd give him the proceeds from the insurance policy, he'd make sure I got a great return on my investment."

Kelly and Mike didn't say anything; they just listened to the distraught woman.

"I got a call from Carlos late this afternoon demanding the money he said Jeff owed him. I asked him how I could be sure he wouldn't call again, demanding more money from me. He told me he was wanted in the United States for murder and that it was very dangerous for him to even be here and that he couldn't risk it again. He said I would have to take his word that this would be the last time I would ever hear from him or see him. I didn't have a choice. I told him I had the cash and that I had packed it in a large suitcase. He said he would be here at 9:00 tonight, like I told you when I called you."

"Did Gabe know about Carlos?"

"Yes. I told him Carlos had provided the money to build the marijuana farm Jeff built on the back of the property. I told him how Carlos told me he'd paid for the plants, the irrigation, and furnished the workers. In return, Jeff was to pay Carlos half the profits over the years. When the crop burned to the ground, Carlos demanded his money back. I told him how Carlos had threatened to kill both Brandon and me if I didn't pay him back.

"I knew Carlos was coming tonight and I needed to have a million and a half dollars to pay him off so I told Gabe no, I wouldn't give him the money. He couldn't believe it when I showed him the suitcase stuffed with the cash. He screamed and yelled at me and demanded that I give him the money, telling me that if I really loved him I'd trust him with it. I told him it wasn't that at all, I just wasn't ready to make such a big decision on such short notice. I told him I needed some time to think about it. I said I needed to have the money to pay off Carlos before I did anything with the rest of the money. We had a big argument and when he left the house he was furious." She started sobbing.

Kelly turned to Mike. "Well, that explains why Gabe killed Carlos. He didn't want him to have any of Marcy's money. He needed it all. It also explains why he killed Jeff. It was pretty much what we'd talked about. He thought he would either gain access to the right to develop the ranch into a hotel and spa or he would get Marcy to give him the insurance money. Either way he gets out of the financial jam he was in."

She turned back to Marcy, "I hate to tell you this, but I think you need to know that Gabe was planning on killing you so he could get the insurance money. Before Mike arrived and while I was outside the shack, right after he killed Carlos, he started swearing and I overheard him say 'Marcy, get back out there. I need that money and the only way I'm going to get it from you is when you're dead.' He knew you'd packed half of the insurance settlement cash in the suitcase you were going to give to Carlos. I'm sure his plan was that after he killed you he would go to your house and steal the suitcase with the cash in it as well as all the rest of the cash from the insurance settlement. It would be easy for him to do as it would only take a couple of minutes for him to stop at the ranch house and grab the money.

"Gabe would be free to walk out the front door with three million dollars in cash and no one would ever know he had even been here. His financial problems would be solved, just like that. The authorities, meaning Sheriff Mike, would probably think it was a professional gangland style hit aimed at Carlos by some Mexican drug cartel and you just got in the way so they took you out too. It would look like the cartel assassin grabbed the cash and was probably back in Mexico. You're safe now. No one can hurt you. Carlos is dead and Gabe is in jail. I'll stay with you tonight until your sister gets here," Kelly said, putting her arm around Marcy.

"You both must think I'm a fool," Marcy said, sobbing. "The thing is, I really loved Gabe and I thought he loved me. I've loved him since we were engaged before I met Jeff. I was heartbroken when he broke up with me and married that woman in Sunset Bay. I married Jeff on the rebound. My life has become a living nightmare."

"Marcy, we don't think you're a fool at all. Please go on and tell us what happened," Mike said.

She took a deep breath and continued, "That's about it. I called Gabe several times on his cell phone after he left this evening. I wanted to apologize to him, but he had his phone turned off. A few minutes before the time Carlos told me he'd be here, I heard a car pull into the driveway. A moment later I heard a gunshot, and then I opened the front door and saw Carlos lying on the ground, obviously dead. I started to go to him when your deputy yelled at me to get back in the house. The deputy knelt down behind his car. That's just about everything."

"Here, Marcy. Take these aspirin. As hard as you've been crying, you're going to have a horrible headache," Kelly said, taking a bottle of aspirin out of her purse.

"Does Brandon have to know about this? It will kill him to think his father was dealing with a Mexican drug cartel mobster and that his mother always loved Gabe and not his father."

Mike was silent for a few moments before he answered her. "Marcy, it will be public knowledge that Gabe killed both Jeff and Carlos. I can't do anything about that. It will probably come out that Carlos was trying to get money from you and that Jeff owed him some money. That's not unusual. Often there's bad blood when business deals don't work out, particularly when there's some sort of criminal enterprise involved. Hopefully, the reason Jeff owed him money can be kept sealed. There's a good chance Gabe's lawyer will agree to a plea bargain and the case will never proceed to a public trial. As far as you loving Gabe while you were married to Jeff, I don't think there's any reason for that to come out. A good case could be made that Gabe loved you and was jealous when he overheard you talking to Carlos on the phone and making an appointment to see him tonight. If the case doesn't go to a public trial, I think we could say that Gabe was jealous and that was the reason he killed Carlos. Kelly, what do you think?"

"I think the less Brandon has to deal with, the better. There's no reason to call him tonight. Marcy, I can call him tomorrow for you if you'd like, or you can call him, or maybe your sister could. What happened here is not really relevant to him, other than it happened on property he now owns. Does that sound about right to both of you?"

Mike and Marcy both nodded. Mike stood up, put on his Stetson, and walked over to the door. "Kelly, I've got to get the paperwork done on Gabe and oversee the call to his attorney. Rebel and I will be home later. You're going to stay here until Marcy's sister comes, right?"

"Yes. I'll see you at home."

"Marcy," Mike said, "when you've had a little time to process everything that's happened tonight, I think you're going to be pretty grateful you had the presence of mind to call me earlier tonight and tell me Carlos was coming to the ranch. And remember, a fool wouldn't have done that."

He walked out the door and saw that the coroner was getting ready to transport Carlos' body to the morgue. The front yard and the driveway were filled with crime scene investigators gathering evidence. Marcy and Kelly overheard Mike say to one of the investigators, "I'm pretty sure this 30-30 rifle is the murder weapon. I picked it up with my handkerchief so the prints on it should be Gabe Lewis'. I think if you compare the bullet that killed Carlos to a sample bullet fired from this gun, you'll find they match. I think you'll also find a match with the bullet that killed Jeff Black."

CHAPTER TWENTY-TWO

Kelly stayed with Marcy until her sister got to the ranch shortly after midnight. It was well past her usual bedtime when she was finally able get to bed with just a few hours for sleep before she had to get up and be at the coffee shop by 6:00 a.m. As the first light of dawn crept into the bedroom, she looked over at Mike who was sleeping peacefully beside her. He'd been asleep when she'd come home late last night.

I'll get more of the details about what happened with Gabe when I see him later today or this evening. Poor Marcy. It must have been devastating to find out the man you've loved for twenty years was going to kill you. Plus, he was the man who destroyed her marriage and caused her to become dependent on her son's benevolence. I'll never understand why people make some of the choices they do. Of course, it's always a lot easier to sit back and Monday morning quarterback when it's not you it's happening to. Thank heavens I've never been in Marcy's situation.

Roxie, Madison, and Charlie were waiting for her at the coffee shop door when she pulled into the parking lot. She was barraged with questions from them as soon as she was within earshot.

"I haven't talked to Mike this morning, so I really can't comment on what happened last night. And I'd like to know how the three of you already seem to know a lot about what happened out at Black's ranch last night."

"Kelly, it used to be that we Indians communicated with one another by using tom-toms to get the word out. Now it's as simple as a cell phone call," Charlie said. "Glad the whole thing is over and everyone will know that no tribal members were involved in Jeff Black's murder. I know we were under suspicion."

"I can't comment on that, but I can tell you that there is conclusive proof that no tribe member was involved and I'm glad. I've come to really like your dad, Chief Many Trees."

"Yeah, he feels the same way. Said he just might make you an honorary member of the tribe since, from what we hear, you cleared us of any involvement."

"Sorry, but no comment," she said as she unlocked the door and the four of them entered the coffee shop. In just a few moments the smell of coffee permeated the coffee shop and the lights cut through the semi-darkness of the early morning hour, bathing the coffee shop and the pier in a soft warm glow. "Better get ready for a busy day. You know how it is. Any time something major happens in this town, everyone wants to come to Kelly's Koffee Shop and talk about it. Think this is going to be one of those days."

Kelly was right. Charlie cooked non-stop while Kelly and Roxie took orders and served them continuously throughout the morning. "Wish this was one of those mornings when Madison didn't have classes at her cosmetology school. Too bad she had to leave to go there. I sure could use her now," Kelly said to Roxie as the two of them almost collided when they both tried to go through the swinging kitchen doors at the same time.

"I know, but from what she tells me, she loves it, and she's really doing well. Sounds like life is looking up for the kid now that her dad's stopped drinking and she's become involved with the church. I couldn't be happier for her. She deserves to have something good in her life," Roxie said.

"No argument there, plus she's a huge help to me. I guess she's going to start helping out Wanda at her beauty shop in the afternoons after she finishes work here at the coffee shop. Imagine she'll start working there when she gets her license. They do grow up, don't they? Guess I'll have to look for a replacement in a few months," Kelly said as she walked into the kitchen to check on some orders.

Roxie stuck her head through the doors. "Kelly, Mike just pulled up. Thought you'd want to know."

"Thanks, Roxie." She walked out of the kitchen and saw him just as he was opening the front door. She waved him over. "Better grab that table. It's been crazy all morning and the lunchtime group will start arriving any minute now." She looked up as the door again opened. "See, I was right. Doc's always the first one here." She waved to Doc and Lucky, motioning them over.

"Doc, you're just in time to hear what happened last night. And this must be Lucky," Mike said, bending down to the pet the little puppy. Rebel had walked over to Mike as soon as he opened the door and put his paw on Mike's leg as if to say, "What about me? I could use some petting or an ear scratch."

"Yeah, when I went to the clinic this morning I heard there was a little excitement out at the Black's ranch last night. Kind of figured you two were involved. What happened?"

Mike filled Doc in on the events of the previous evening at Black's ranch. "Kelly, got time to sit for a minute?" Mike said. "I need to bring you up to date on what's happening. Doc, you can stay if you want."

"I'll make time," Kelly said. "Just give me a minute to tell Roxie I'm taking a break." She walked over to Roxie and then hurried back to the table. "Shoot. I'm all ears. Don't leave anything out. You were sound asleep when I got home last night and I didn't want to wake you up this morning."

"After I left you last night I drove to the jail. Rich had put Gabe in a jail cell and he was screaming and yelling that he wanted to call his lawyer, so I let him make a phone call. Surprisingly, he called his wife, not his lawyer. Guess he decided he'd rather get out of jail first and then talk to his lawyer. Long story short, he told his wife he'd been arrested and he was in jail. Said she needed to come over to Cedar Bay immediately and bail him out. She refused. Rich and I could overhear her tell him he could stay there for the rest of his life for all she cared. She told him she'd call his attorney for him."

"Wow!" Kelly said. "That took some courage. I'd heard that she'd talked to her lawyer about getting a divorce. Guess she's going through with it."

"That would be my guess," Mike said. "Gabe spent the night in jail and he was not a happy man. His lawyer came this morning and talked to him. I don't know what they said to one another because that's privileged information, but it must have had something to do with Gabe's financial problems, because he's still in jail. He hasn't made bail yet."

"What happens now?" Doc asked.

"Well, he's being arraigned this afternoon and he'll no doubt plead not guilty. If he still can't make bail, he'll go back to jail until he's tried for murder or his attorney negotiates a plea bargain with the District Attorney. Either way, I don't think we'll be seeing much of Gabe Lewis for a long time."

"Have you talked to Marcy this morning?" Kelly asked.

"Yes. She called to thank me for saving her life. She sounded much better than last night. She told me she was going to Portland to stay with her sister until the holidays, and then she planned on coming back to the ranch so Brandon could spend the holidays at the home he's always known. She said she and Brandon needed to decide what they were going to do about everything. Since the ranch and all the money with the exception of the insurance proceeds are Brandon's now, don't know exactly what that means."

"I'm so glad it's over and you can take it easy for awhile.

Remember, we've got a lot more planning to do for the wedding."

"What are you talking about? We decided when, where, and who's going to be in it. You've got your dress. What more is there to do?"

Kelly stared at him in disbelief, shook her head, stood up, and started to walk over to the cash register. She turned back and kissed the top of Mike's head. "Sweetheart, I know you think finding killers is tough. Trust me, it's a piece of cake compared to planning a wedding."

"Mike," Doc said, laughing, "I'm a doctor and I have to tell you, you're not looking all that well at this moment. The next couple of months may be a very interesting time for you."

*****

"Kelly, the phone's for you," Madison said that afternoon as she helped Roxie clean up.

"Thanks, Madison. Who is it?"

"Don't know. Didn't recognize the woman's voice."

"This is Kelly Conner."

"Kelly, we haven't met, but I feel I know you very well. My name is Jackie Lewis. I'm Gabe Lewis' wife."

Kelly wasn't sure what she was expected to say. This was unchartered territory and a call she never expected to receive. "Jackie, I didn't have the pleasure of meeting you when I was at Lewis Kennels the other day, but Angie was so helpful and the friend I gave the yellow lab to is thrilled with the puppy."

"I'm glad to hear that. I love my dogs. I understand that you're responsible for my husband being in jail, is that correct?"

Good grief, Kelly thought. *I'm glad this is only a phone call and not a personal meeting. I don't think this is going to be pleasant.* She took a deep breath and answered, "That is somewhat correct. I was there when your husband was arrested by the sheriff and it's true that I'm partly responsible for him being in jail."

"Well, you may think this is strange, but I'm calling to thank you. I was planning on divorcing Gabe and had met with my attorney to start the proceedings. As a matter of fact, even though he's in jail, he's going to be served with the divorce papers today. Rather ironic, don't you think? Anyway, from what his attorney told me when he called and wanted money from me to bail Gabe out of jail, it sounds like he'll be going to prison for a long time."

"I think that's probably a fair assessment. I understand Gabe is still in jail, so I gather you didn't arrange for him to get out of jail on bail."

"No. After all I've put up with him from one affair after another, his lies, his cheating, and his inept handling of his business affairs, this is karmic justice. He deserves whatever he gets. I met Marcy Black once and tried to convince her that Gabe was not the man he told her he was. She didn't believe me. I don't envy her. From what I hear, she's suffered a lot of losses lately. It's strange, but I feel the best I've felt in a long time. I feel free and it's a new, refreshing feeling for me. Now I can concentrate on my dogs and the kennels. I'm even thinking of expanding my kennel business."

"I understood from Angie that your dogs are your passion."

"They are. I have three of my own and every time a litter is born, I feel like I have new little babies. Sounds crazy, but yes, they are my passion. Speaking of that, is there any chance you could come out to the kennel this afternoon? I have a thank you present for you."

"Jackie, you don't need to give me anything. I'm just glad that something good is coming out of this."

"Well, I know I don't need to give you anything, but I would like to thank you in person. How about four this afternoon?"

"All right. I'll see you then." *Well, that turned out a whole lot different than I thought it would. Wonder why she was so insistent I meet her at the kennel this afternoon.*

Later that afternoon Kelly drove up the tree-lined driveway to Lewis Kennels and saw the same car that had been at Marcy's several days earlier, the SUV with Lewis Kennels written in bold white letters on it. Her tires crunched on the gravel as she pulled into the parking place in front of the office. Almost immediately Angie and another woman walked out the door.

"You must be Kelly," the attractive woman said, holding out her hand. "I'm Jackie. Thanks for coming. I apologize for my appearance. I was cleaning up one of the kennels and I'm sure I look like a mess." Her jeans and blue denim shirt were stained and Kelly could see some strands of hay that had gotten caught in the long braid that hung down her back. "I've got something I want to show you. Please, come with me."

Kelly followed her into the yellow lab kennel where she'd bought Lucky. If possible, it seemed like there were even more dogs than there had been a few days earlier. Jackie walked down the center aisle to the back of the kennel and stopped in front of a wire enclosure. Inside was the most beautiful puppy Kelly had ever seen. It sat looking up at her with large chocolate brown eyes. Kelly knelt down and held out her hand, palm down. The puppy gently licked it and then held its paw out to Kelly. She took it in her hand and turned to look up at Jackie. "She's beautiful. I wish I had someone who needed her."

"From what I heard, you might just be the perfect candidate for a new puppy. I heard you have a big beautiful boxer who's pretty much been your guard dog. I also heard that the boxer is becoming attached to your fiancé and you need a little more feminine energy in your house. This little girl is a gift from me to you. You've done more for me than you'll ever know and this is one small way for me to say thank you."

Jackie opened the door of the wire enclosure, walked in, and scooped the beautiful puppy up in her arms. She turned around and handed her to Kelly. "Her dam was the best in class at Westminster and her sire placed first in the Canadian dog show that's on par with Westminster. Her lineage is impeccable. She'll make a great family dog or she might just help you in some of the other things I hear you do. She's one of the smartest little dogs I've ever had."

Kelly held the squirming little yellow bundle of fur in her arms as tears started to flow down her cheeks. "Jackie, where did you hear all this about me? This seems to be a lot more than random guessing on your part."

"Well, a little birdie by the name of Sheriff Mike told me when I called to thank him for arresting Gabe. I told him I wanted to do something for him and that's when he told me about you. He said to tell you it was a wedding present from him to you and no, I refused to be paid for the dog. I just want the dog to have a good home and I'm certain she will."

"I'm totally speechless and from what people say about me, that doesn't happen very often. Thank you so much."

Jackie reached out her hand and stroked the little puppy. "Have a good life, little girl." She turned away, her eyes glistening.

Kelly walked out the door to the minivan where a dog bed and puppy food had been placed next to it. Angie waved as Kelly carefully put the puppy in the dog bed and placed it in the back seat.

Well, some days you just never know what's going to happen in your life and this is definitely one of those days. She heard a contented sigh coming from the back seat as she turned the minivan south towards Cedar Bay.

RECIPES

CALICO BEAN BAKE

½ pound hamburger
½ pound bacon (cut in 1" pieces)
1 cup chopped onion
½ cup catsup
1 teaspoon salt
½ cup brown sugar
1 teaspoon mustard
1 16 oz. can kidney beans
1 16 oz. can butter beans
1 16 oz. can pork and beans

Preheat oven to 350 degrees.

Brown the hamburger and bacon. Add chopped onion and cook until soft and translucent. Place the mixture in an ovenproof casserole dish. Stir in the catsup, salt, sugar, and mustard. Drain kidney beans and butter beans and add to the mixture. Add the can of pork and beans, undrained, to the mixture. Stir mixture until all ingredients are evenly distributed. Bake for 40 minutes. Enjoy!

MORMOR'S GRAVLAX

1 salmon filet, approximately 3 lbs
1 large bunch of dill (reserve a few sprigs for garnish)
¼ cup kosher salt
¼ cup sugar
2 tablespoons crushed peppercorns (I crush them in a small food processor)
1 tablespoon whole fennel seeds
Pumpernickel bread, cocktail size rye bread, or crackers for serving
Optional – diced red onion, diced hard-boiled egg, capers

Remove any bones that may be in the filet using a pair of needle nose pliers or tweezers. Cut the salmon filet in half crosswise and place half of it, skin side down, in a flat deep dish. Wash and pat the dill dry and place it on top of the filet. Combine the salt, sugar, peppercorns, and fennel seeds in a small bowl and sprinkle them evenly over the filet. Place the other half of the salmon on top, skin side up. Cover the dish with aluminum foil. Place a pan weighted with food cans on top of the foil. Refrigerate the salmon for two days, turning the fish every 12 hours. Baste with the liquid that will accumulate in the bottom of the dish.

Drain the liquid and wipe the fish clean. Using a sharp thin knife, slice the salmon filets across the grain in long thin slices, removing the skin as you cut it. Arrange the slices on a serving platter. Cover with plastic wrap and refrigerate. When ready to serve, surround the salmon with bread or crackers and place the mustard sauce in the center. Scatter the chopped, reserved dill, on top of the thinly sliced salmon. You may also sprinkle the optional diced red onion, diced hard-boiled egg, and capers on top.

MUSTARD SAUCE

¼ cup Dijon mustard
1 teaspoon ground dry mustard
3 tablespoons sugar
2 tablespoons white wine vinegar

1/3 cup olive oil
3 tablespoons chopped fresh dill

Combine the mustards, sugar, and vinegar in a small bowl. Slowly whisk in the olive oil and stir in the chopped dill. Serve chilled with the gravlax. Enjoy!

DUTCH RICHARDS KILLER CHOCOLATE CAKE

2 cups plain flour
2 cups sugar
1 teaspoon baking soda
2 sticks unsalted butter
4 tablespoons cocoa
1 cup water
2 eggs, lightly beaten
½ cup buttermilk
1 teaspoon vanilla extract

Preheat oven to 350 degrees.

Stir together the flour, sugar, and baking soda. Set aside.

Combine the butter, cocoa, and water in a saucepan. Bring to a boil. Add the melted butter mixture to the dry ingredients and mix well. Add the eggs, buttermilk, and vanilla. Use electric beater to combine ingredients thoroughly. Lightly grease a 9" x 13" baking dish and dust with flour. Pour the mixed ingredients into the dish. Bake for 20 minutes. If the middle of the cake is wiggly, continue baking. Check every five minutes. Baking time varies with ovens. Don't over bake.

CHOCOLATE ICING

1 stick unsalted butter
4 tablespoons cocoa
6 tablespoons buttermilk

16 oz. box powdered sugar
1 teaspoon vanilla extract
Optional – chopped nuts

Combine the butter, cocoa, and buttermilk in a saucepan. Bring to a boil. Beat in sugar, vanilla, and nuts if desired. Pour evenly over the hot cake and let cool. Enjoy!

CARAMEL OVERNIGHT ROLLS

1 15 oz. package frozen dinner roll dough
1 large package dry butterscotch pudding (not instant)
½ cup packed brown sugar
½ stick (8 tablespoons) unsalted butter, melted
Optional: chopped pecans

Lightly grease a 10-12 cup Bundt pan.

Arrange individual balls of dough in the pan, evenly stacking one on top of another. Sprinkle each layer of the balls of dough first with the dry pudding mix, then the brown sugar.

Pour melted butter over the top and scatter with chopped pecans, if desired.

Cover with a towel and let rise overnight, unrefrigerated.

When ready to cook the rolls, preheat the oven to 325 degrees. Cook for 30 – 35 minutes. Remove from oven and let stand for five minutes. Place a plate on top of pan and flip over. Slide the pan up and off the rolls. Cut or pull off individual rolls and serve. Enjoy!

BREAKFAST TART

1 sheet frozen puff pastry dough, thawed
1 egg, lightly beaten combined with 1 teaspoon water (egg wash)
3 ounces crème fraiche (if you can't find it, substitute 1 cup sour

cream or 1 cup plain yogurt
    2 ounces Gruyere cheese, shredded (I often substitute Jarlsberg or
    Swiss because it's cheaper)
    Salt and pepper to taste
    8 bacon slices, cooked until crisp
    4 eggs
    10 fresh chives, cut on the bias into ½" lengths

Preheat oven to 425 degrees. Lightly grease a baking sheet with raised sides.

On a lightly floured surface, roll out the pasty to approximately a 1/2" thickness and cut into a 10" x 8" rectangle. Place the pastry on the prepared baking sheet. Using a paring knife, lightly score the border ½" in from the edge of the pastry. Using a fork, prick the center of the pastry about 10 times. Brush the border with the egg wash and refrigerate for 15 minutes.

In a small bowl, combine the crème fraiche and the cheese. Season with the salt and pepper.

Spread crème fraiche mixture on the pastry, keeping the border clean. Lay the bacon on top and slightly overlap the slices. Bake the tart 15 minutes, rotating the baking sheet halfway through. Remove the baking sheet from the oven. Using a fork, prick any large air pockets on the pastry. Crack the eggs onto the tart, spacing them about 2" apart. Bake until egg whites are set and yolks are still soft, approximately 7 – 10 minutes. Transfer the tart to a platter and garnish with the chives. Serve and enjoy!

ABOUT THE AUTHOR

Dianne lives in Huntington Beach, California with her husband Tom, a former California State Senator, and is a frequent contributor to the Huffington Post. Her other award winning books include:

Kelly's Koffee Shop

Blue Coyote Motel
Coyote in Provence
Cornered Coyote

Tea Party Teddy
Tea Party Teddy's Legacy

Website: www.dianneharman.com
Blog: www.dianneharman.com/blog
Email: dianne@dianneharman.com

Made in the USA
Lexington, KY
03 January 2015